Dear America

The Diary of
Dawnie Rae Johnson

With the Might
of Angels

ANDREA DAVIS PINKNEY

SCHOLASTIC INC. ◆ NEW YORK

This book is dedicated to the legacies of
Thurgood Marshall and George E. Bragg.

Copyright © 2011 by Andrea Davis Pinkney

All rights reserved. Published by Scholastic Inc., *Publishers since 1920.*
SCHOLASTIC, DEAR AMERICA, and associated logos are trademarks and/or registered
trademarks of Scholastic Inc. No part of this publication may be reproduced,
stored in a retrieval system, or transmitted in any form or by any means,
electronic, mechanical, photocopying, recording, or otherwise, without written
permission of the publisher. For information regarding permission, write to
Scholastic Inc., Attention: Permissions Department,
557 Broadway, New York, NY 10012.

Library of Congress Cataloging-in-Publication Data

Pinkney, Andrea Davis.
With the might of angels : the diary of Dawnie Rae Johnson /
Andrea Davis Pinkney. — 1st ed.
p. cm. — (Dear America)
Summary: In 1955 Hadley, Virginia, twelve-year-old Dawnie Rae Johnson, a
tomboy who excels at baseball and at her studies, becomes the first African
American student to attend the all-white Prettyman Coburn school, turning
her world upside down. Includes historical notes about the period.
ISBN 978-0-545-29705-9
[1. School integration—Fiction. 2. Schools—Fiction. 3. Race relations—Fiction.
4. African Americans—Fiction. 5. Family life—Virginia—Fiction. 6. Diaries—
Fiction. 7. Virginia—History—20th century—Fiction.] I. Title.
PZ7.P6333Wi 2011
[Fic]—dc22

2011001363

10 9 8 7 6 5 4 3 2 1   11 12 13 14 15

The text type was set in ITC Legacy Serif.
The display type was set in House-A-Rama League Night.
Book design by Kevin Callahan

Printed in the U.S.A. 23
First edition, September 2011

Hadley, Virginia

1954

Diary Book,

It's early, before the sun even knows she's got sleep in her eyes. With the way the heat is already rising, Mama will no doubt say this morning is as hot as the day I was born.

Folks in Lee County still talk about me coming into this world. "Someday you'll put it in a book," Daddy likes to say.

Well, thanks to Goober, I now have a book to write in.

The best way to tell about something is from the beginning. Even in a diary book that's private, and for my eyes only, it's good for me to write about myself from the start — to claim this book as really, truly mine. In case anyone ever finds my diary, they'll know about me.

Mama said I was born right as the new day was dawning. Came into this world during the "in-between," when night is changing to day, when morning starts to roll out like a pie crust. That's why Mama and Daddy named me Dawn, after the in-between.

When Mama cradled me for the first time, she put my name to a song. *"Dawnie, Dawnie, sweet potato pie."*

The nickname stuck—Dawnie.

My middle name, Rae, is the name Mama had before she married Daddy. She was Loretta Rae then. She's Loretta Johnson now, the name of Daddy's people, and my name, too. Dawnie Rae Johnson.

When I was born, I came on strong like the sun, and, Mama says, "Loudest baby to ever cry in Hadley Hospital."

"You were shouting good news," says Daddy. "You've been blessed with the gift of gab ever since."

One thing about being born when the sun's about to rise—and being named after that time of day—is that I always beat the morning. When my eyes are wide open, the sun is still deciding to sleep for five minutes more.

This morning when I woke, I was hard-pressed to wait even five minutes for anything. The first chorus of bullfinches were welcoming May with their song. Seems those happy birds knew it was my birthday. And thanks to Goober, my celebrating had already started.

As soon as I felt this hard, flat square pressing up through my pillow, I knew Goober had done something special. Goober is *some* little brother.

4

He can sure rattle me plenty, but he knows how to make me happy, too. Only eight years old, and full of surprises. During the morning's in-between, I yanked this diary book out from under my half-'sleep head.

When I got to the kitchen, I was all smiles. Goober was there with Mama and Daddy. He'd lined up his peanut shells along the edge of our kitchen table, nose-to-tail, in a parade.

Most likely it was Goober who'd propped my pogo stick on one side of my chair, and my baseball bat on the other.

Goober spotted the book in my hand right off.

"Dawnie," he said, "I made it for you special. It's a diary for your birthday."

Special is sure right. This diary is small and square, and put together like two slices of dark toast pressed into a sandwich. Its spine has been sewn with thick twine. The pages are rough at the edges, but there are plenty of them for writing. I named my birthday gift as soon as I held it—Diary Book. Thick as a brick, and sure hefty. Lots of gristle on this book's bones. Just like me.

At breakfast, I ran my fingers along my diary's bumpy spine.

"You *made* this?" I said to Goober.

"Mama helped me," Goober said.

"We know how much you like to write." Mama looked as proud as Goober.

Goober rocked in his chair, set the chair's back legs up to tilting. Then he handed me another gift: a new red pencil, with a plump eraser.

"For the bestest sister," Goober said.

"*You're* the bestest, Goober," I said, then hugged him. "Thank you."

I sure don't know why people say Goober is slow. I think he's as regular as anybody, only different in certain ways. Mama's tried to explain it to me, but I have a hard time understanding. "Your brother's one of God's beautiful creatures. *You* came here with the gift of talk. Goober's gift is that he sees the world in his own way."

There's nothing wrong with Goober's eyesight. Sometimes he won't look at you when he speaks. But my brother can no doubt see fine.

Some kids say Goober's addle-brained. Others say he's touched in the head, or a simpleton. To me, Goober's just special.

My little brother's given name is Gunther Johnson. But the boy loves peanuts, so we've been forever calling him Goober. Most days his pockets bulge with peanuts and their shells. His skin is the same brown as a peanut, too. "And he's just as pudgy." My daddy always winks when he says this.

Daddy works nights mostly, hauling and loading milk casks and cheese crates from the backs of trucks at Sutter's Dairy, the biggest dairy supply in all of Lee County.

Daddy leaves for work after supper, returns right before morning, eats breakfast with us, then reads his stack of newspapers before he sleeps. This morning, like always, Daddy was deep in his reading. Didn't look up once. That's Daddy. He reads like words on a page are the tastiest plate of grits ever.

"You get that from him, Dawnie," Mama says. "The two of you read faster than drinking root beer through a straw. And you, child, take in book learning just as quickly."

Mama's right. At school I'm quicker than most kids.

Daddy can't get enough of his newspapers and magazines. He stacks them all next to his coffee cup — *Look*, an NAACP journal called *The Crisis*, and our local paper, the *Hadley Register*. Daddy even somehow gets his hands on that

Northerner newspaper the *New York Times*.

This morning when I sat down, Daddy took a break from his breakfast reading. The little smile playing in his eyes told me a surprise was brewing. He studied me for a long moment. "Happy birthday, Dawnie."

Then he pushed that New York paper under my nose. "Here, child."

He was eager to show me the front-page headline. "Clip this for your new diary."

I looked carefully.

Daddy told me to read what I saw. He said, "Speak loud enough to scare some pigeons."

I read slowly, pressing each word into the warm morning air.

Seems Mama already knew the news.

Didn't take her but a minute to hand me a pair of scissors from her sewing basket and a tin of paste from her craft bin.

"Make your birthday book look pretty," Goober said.

Nobody even had to tell me what to do. I knew right off why those scissors and paste brush were suddenly in my hands.

I've carefully glued the headline right here as a memory of the day I turned twelve.

**HIGH COURT BANS
SCHOOL SEGREGATION;**

**9-TO-0 DECISION
GRANTS TIME
TO COMPLY**

Washington, May 17

Wednesday, May 19, 1954
Diary Book,

I want to tell you everything. I could write all night about today, but Mama has already given me two warnings. "Dawnie, lights off. It's past nine o'clock!"

At school, kids and teachers were talking about integration, and what it said in that New York paper. I even heard our principal, Mr. Calhoun, say, "An ice storm will fall on the tropics before any white folks let us into their schools."

I could write more, but Mama's calling for the third time. "Dawnie, turn off that light!" I'll put you under my pillow where I first found you. You can share the spot with my birthday candle, the last one to lose its flame from my blowing. Mama says the final candle to go out is the one that makes your wish come true.

9

I'll be back at you soon, Diary Book.

Catch you during the in-between.

Thursday, May 20, 1954

Diary Book,

Today Yolanda and me didn't come right home after school, like we're supposed to. I mean, this *is* my birthday week, and I *did* make a wish on the candles Mama had put on my cake at supper on Tuesday. I didn't need those candles for wishing, though. I've had the same wish for as long as I can remember — to see the inside of Prettyman Coburn, Hadley's white school.

Mama and Daddy have told me time and again that I am never to go to the white part of town without them.

Daddy once said, "If I ever get wind of you going over there, your behind will wonder if it can grow skin again."

But I wasn't really going to be *in* the white part of town, I was just passing *by* the white part of town so that I could see Prettyman.

Yolanda and me took the long way home. Really, it wasn't even *on* the way home, but it *was* long. Truth be told (since this is my diary, I can be honest), Prettyman is way on the other side of Hadley, nowhere near to where we live.

By walking the main streets, it takes just about one whole hour to walk the two miles to Prettyman from our neighborhood. It's less than half that time when you take shortcuts.

Even though this was the long way home, it was the shortest way to get to Prettyman. Yolanda and I walked along Weedle Lane, which brought us through the piney woods, up behind Prettyman, where the sports field meets the railroad tracks. The grass is high and yellow there, and thick with weeds. I had my pogo stick stretched across the backs of my shoulders, arms hung over each end.

I nudged Yolanda. "Look at that baseball field!" I said.

"It's like something from a movie," Yolanda said.

I blinked. "They even have a dugout."

"And padded bases," Yolanda said.

We stayed low in the grasses.

I saw a girl come out Prettyman's back door and unlatch a bell from a hook on the school's bricks. She looked to be my same age. She walked around the side of the building to the front, holding the bell. The bell was no bigger than a teacup, but when she waved it, it sure clanged loudly. That bell's sound was as beautiful as the sight of the baseball field.

"You hear that, Dawnie?"

"They must ring that same bell when you step off a cloud to enter heaven," I said.

Saturday, May 22, 1954
Diary Book,

I'm as awake as a hooty owl on this black night, thinking about Prettyman's baseball field. I've been trying to sleep, but over and over, I keep seeing the same moving picture in my mind: Me, Dawnie Rae, rounding the bases on Prettyman's baseball diamond. Can you imagine anything better? I wouldn't be surprised if those bases were made of *real* diamonds.

Here are a few more things I want to write about me, to make this diary truly mine. Folks call me a "hay girl," or a "coal catcher." That's the same as calling me a tomboy. People can say what they want. They're mostly right in thinking I'm not scared of getting dirty. Hay and coal don't bother me. Neither do dirt, night crawlers, bugs, or even the smell of rotten eggs.

Running fast and hard makes me happier than

a grasshopper at a jump-rope contest, and I swim as good as any frog.

I'm nimble, too. I can wrestle a knot free from a tangle of shoelaces, trap a moth by its wing with two of my fingers, and clear the hedge that separates our yard from Marietta Street, where we live.

I've never liked dresses or shoes that shine. Even if I were going to meet President Dwight D. Eisenhower himself, I'd show up to shake his hand in dungarees and Keds. Don't stick me in starched skirts or anything with a ruffle, except on Sundays when Mama insists that I look "correct" for church.

As much as it hurts to wear one of the three dresses or two skirts I own, I do it sometimes for Mama and Daddy, and for Goober, who likes to say, "Dresses show your strong ankles, Dawnie."

What's really "correct" is what suits a person best. And what suits me is playing baseball. More than anything, I want to be part of the All-American Girls Baseball League, a group of women baseball players. But there are no Negroes playing in the AAGBBL. Not a single one.

Someday I will write a letter to Jackie Robinson, second baseman for the Brooklyn Dodgers, and the first Negro baseball player to play in the modern major leagues, to see if he can help get me into the AAGBBL.

If anybody would know how to break in, Jackie would. Used to be that Major League Baseball didn't allow colored players. Jackie changed all that. He stepped over what folks called "the color line," and added some *color* to the major leagues.

Anyway, for now, I'll have to keep batting in Orem's Pasture, down past Yolanda's house at the place where Ebert Street meets up with Landleton Avenue.

Monday, May 24, 1954
Diary Book,

Things at school are getting stranger and stranger. I'm glad we've only got a few weeks to go before summer break.

Today Mr. Calhoun called me and two other kids into his office. Yolanda, Roger Wilkes, and I slid onto the bench that faced Mr. Calhoun's desk.

Mr. Calhoun was looking mostly at me, it seems. Before he could even speak, I defended myself for what I thought I'd done bad. "Mr. Calhoun, I swear, the only reason I brought my pogo stick into school today was because yesterday when I left it out, there was bird plop all over the handle. Geese are coming back to Virginia from farther south, and they're having a welcome home party."

Yolanda looked at me sideways. She was wearing a smirk. "Geese make big plops," she said.

Roger snickered, but I really didn't see what was so funny. Yolanda was sticking up for me, and she was only telling the truth.

Mr. Calhoun didn't think it was funny, either. He was serious when he said to me, "Dawnie, you have the highest grades in the elementary division at Mary McLeod Bethune School, and as such, we'd like you to give a speech for the sixth-grade Stepping Up ceremony next month."

I know I have good grades, but giving speeches — that's not me. I answered with a question. "How come Yolanda and Roger are here?"

Mr. Calhoun was quick to answer. "The three of you are our best and brightest students, and we'd like each of you to speak at the Stepping Up ceremony. Yolanda and Roger will say a few words. As the highest-ranking student, you, Dawnie, will deliver a speech."

Yolanda bumped me with her leg. Roger was

shaking his head, like he was being asked to walk on fire.

"Additionally," said Mr. Calhoun, "we'll be administering a special academic test to each of you to assess your full abilities as you enter seventh grade."

I don't mind school tests, in the same way that baiting a fishhook doesn't bother me. But it's the end of the school year, and I'm sick of studying, and it doesn't seem fair that we have to take a test, seeing as the three of us are the smartest kids at Bethune.

Right then I was wishing I was getting in trouble for my ploppy pogo stick. At least a scolding would be over as soon as we left Mr. Calhoun's office.

Mr. Calhoun explained that the test would be given in four parts, each for a different area of study, and that we'd take the test in one hour segments after school, beginning next week. At the same time, at home in the evenings, we're to work on our remarks for the Stepping Up program.

Roger and Yolanda started to grumble quietly.

They had no good reason to complain. They were way luckier than me. They were being asked to "say a few words" at the Stepping Up ceremony.

I would have to give a whole speech! I tried to turn my attention to taking the test, which came to me a little more natural.

Roger raised his hand. "Mr. Calhoun, is the test on stuff we've already learned?"

"It's a standardized test issued by the Department of Education for the state of Virginia. It covers all aspects of the sixth-grade curriculum," Mr. Calhoun said.

"How are we supposed to study?" Yolanda wanted to know.

"Just come prepared to do your best" was Mr. Calhoun's answer.

As much as I tried, I couldn't yank my thoughts away from the ceremony. I asked a question more important than all the questions about the test. "Do I have to wear a dress for the Stepping Up?"

Mr. Calhoun said, "That's up to you, Dawnie."

When we got outside, Yolanda said, "That's up to your mama."

After Suppertime

When I told Mama and Daddy about the Stepping Up ceremony and the test, they were pleased.

"Up, up, up," said Goober. "You can fly, Dawnie."

Daddy said, "You're a Johnson. You'll perform well on that test, and you'll step up proudly at that ceremony."

Mama's words were hard to hear. "I'll go down to Woolworth's tomorrow and buy fabric for a new dress. Two weeks isn't a lot of time, but I can make you something lovely for your Stepping Up speech."

"You can fly, Dawnie," Goober repeated. "Dawnie can fly."

Tuesday, May 25, 1954
Diary Book,

Since what I write is between you and me, I will use your pages for pie-in-the-sky dreaming. My biggest, most pie-in-the-sky wish is to meet Jackie Robinson.

Jackie won't ever get the chance to read you, but I will write him letters right here on your pages. I will tell him what I wish I could say if he knocked on our front door, and stayed for supper.

Dear Mr. Jackie Robinson,

I am the only girl in all of Lee County who loves baseball. I can bat, pitch, and even ump at a game if I have to. Out back, hanging from our yard's biggest tree, there's a rope with a mop head tied to the end of it. My tree mop, I call it.

This is how I've learned to bat. Every chance I get, I swing at that mop head, keeping my eyes pinned to its strings, pushing my bat right up on it to send the mop head swinging.

Mr. Jackie Robinson, I've always wanted to know:

How does it feel to play baseball in front of so many people?

Who taught you how to swing a bat?

When you're on the field, what are you thinking about?

What does Brooklyn look like?

> *Your fan,*
> *Dawnie Rae Johnson*

Wednesday, May 26, 1954
Diary Book,

There are two public schools in Hadley—*ours* and *theirs.*

Our school, Mary McLeod Bethune, is for colored kids only. It includes kindergartners up to twelfth graders. Everybody at Bethune is colored, including the teachers.

When you live in Hadley, and your skin is any shade of dark, you attend Bethune. There are three "divisions" at our school—elementary, middle, and high school. But really, it's all the same—the Negro school, where white kids wouldn't go if it was the last school on God's earth. Bethune is in the colored part of town, the place white folks call "Crow's Nest." I hate this name. I am no ugly blackbird, and I don't live in a nest. I live in a green wood-frame house on Marietta Street, just off Carlton Avenue, a few minutes from Bethune.

Their school, Prettyman Coburn, is for white kids only. It's in the white part of town, the part people call "Ivoryton." I hate this name, too. How come *they* get to live in Ivory, when *we* have to live with crows?

Our school is named after Mary McLeod Bethune, a fine Negro lady who started a black college and gave advice to President Franklin Roosevelt. Good for Mary. She really helped Negroes. But I will only tell this in my diary, because I'm ashamed to admit it out loud—I hate our school.

I mean, I like *going* to school, but I hate the stuff *in* school. At Bethune, everything's broke.

Our pencils are chewed to the bone. The spines on most books are cracked and so raggedy. And how many lessons have I had to piece together because the pages of our books are torn, or missing?

At Bethune, our classrooms are cramped. We stay in the same room all day with the same teacher who teaches us all subjects.

Even though we're not supposed to chew gum in school, underneath the desks there are enough wads of Wrigley's Spearmint to patch the cracks in a whole bathroom. And speaking of bathrooms, the girls' rooms at Bethune stink. The toilets never flush right. The sinks are rust-stained the ugliest brown ever. Even a crow would not want to pee at Bethune.

Bethune's wall clocks haven't worked since I started in kindergarten. It has been 2:45 at Bethune for seven years!

Bethune is a redbrick building that covers two blocks. When it rains, the bricks rain, too. The streets and sidewalks around Bethune fill with red clay streams from the silt powder that's come loose from the school's rickety bricks. I like rain, but sometimes I worry Bethune will melt right into the ground, like syrup on a pancake.

Prettyman Coburn is two miles from where we live. It's double the size of Bethune, and twice as nice.

That school is a limestone castle, and as white as the kids who go there. Like Bethune, Prettyman takes up two blocks. But those are two of the cleanest blocks anywhere, with sidewalks free of cracks and weeds.

The outside of Prettyman Coburn School looks just like its name — pretty. There's a clock on Prettyman's front cornice. A brass clock that tells the time perfectly and is always correct.

That's how it is. Negroes get a stinky school with broken clocks. White kids get a castle.

We pass Prettyman Coburn each Sunday when we drive to church. Every Sunday, I look and look at that white-as-white building, with the big white-as-white doors, and the little pointy trees lining the walk, spreading across the front like the collar on an expensive coat. And every Sunday, I wonder what's inside Prettyman's walls. If the outside is any clue, the kids at that school are getting their book learning with some nice stuff.

I hear they've got a science lab in that pretty school, that you get a different teacher for each subject, and that students move from room to room for their classes. I would give my eyeteeth, and my molars, too, to have a science lab at school. There's even something called a "homeroom" where kids start and end the day. Can you imagine? A classroom like a home?

Thursday, May 27, 1954
Diary Book,

Yolanda and I walk to school together every morning.

Well, Yolanda walks. She carries her books and mine, while I pogo.

This morning I told Yolanda I'd race her.

"No fair," Yolanda said. "You're wearing overalls. I'm in a skirt. I can't run in a skirt. And — I'm carrying a bunch of books."

"I'll give you a head start."

"What if I trip or get my clothes dirty? My ma will put a wooden spoon to me when I get home."

Poor Yolanda. She's as fast a runner as me, but hardly ever gets to run for real, because of wearing skirts and dresses every day. I mean, she can sorta run, like when a car is coming, and we're trying to make it across the street. But that's not fun running.

Today I agreed to walk with Yolanda. "Okay, me and you, together."

Even though Yolanda's feet couldn't run today, her mind was working fast. "We're early, Dawnie," she said. "How about we go again past Prettyman before Bethune, just to see?"

I'd never been by Prettyman in the morning, other than on a Sunday with my family. I'd already disobeyed Mama and Daddy once by going to Ivoryton without them.

"I don't think we should," I said, wanting more than anything to see kids going *into* that pretty building with its pointy trees and diamond fields, all under the morning sun.

"We'll just pass by the back, like before," Yolanda said. "We won't even stop this time to look really. We can just keep walking."

We got near enough to the school to hear the bell that was ringing to welcome the students. The same girl from before was ringing it, too. She looked so proud and happy to be holding that bell.

The bell's rounded tone seemed to be calling me.

Saturday, May 29, 1954
Diary Book,

Mama says there's not enough time to make me a fancy enough dress for the Stepping Up ceremony. So today we went downtown to Millerton's Department Store to buy me a dress.

The whole thing gave me a bad case of the *how comes*. That's when questions pester me and will not let go. The *how comes* are like flies. As soon as one *how come* shows up, more follow.

How come the saleslady at the store wouldn't let me try on any of the clothes? She made Mama hold each dress up in front of me.

Same for the shoes. Mama had to trace my foot on a piece of paper and slip the paper inside the new shoes to see if they'd fit.

I noticed a white girl my same age going in and out of the dressing room, appearing each time with one of the new dresses on, and her feet in new shoes, seeing if they were her size.

How come Mama didn't tell the saleslady that you can't know if something fits unless you put it on your body?

How come Mama hushed me when I started to say this to the saleslady myself?

How come Mama held my hand so tightly the whole time we were in that blasted store? She was near to crushing my fingers in her grip. Alls I could think on was how the blood was being shut off from my pitching hand.

How come Mama's voice changed from strong to scared whenever the saleslady spoke to her?

How come Mama never once looked that saleslady in the eye?

We settled on a pastel dress with a rounded white collar, and black patent leather shoes with an ankle strap. The dress had a label that described it as "Peach Melba."

I stood very still in front of the store mirror, my arms out wide like a scarecrow, while Mama held up the dress and shoes in front of me.

Right then I wanted to do something that would've made Mama punish me from here till forever — I wanted to spit! First on the saleslady, then on the dress. Then on the insides of each patent leather shoe.

I know *how come* I wanted to spit, too — it wasn't fair that I couldn't try the dress on, ugly as it was. It's a good thing I held on to my spit. I don't think there was enough of it inside my mouth to show how mad I was.

The white girl came out of the dressing room wearing the same pastel dress. We both stood in front of the mirror.

"Oh, Mother," squealed the girl. "This dress is dreamy! I'll take it." She was so happy, and twirling in the same dress *my* mama was buying for *me*.

How come the white girl's mother told her they would *not* be buying the pastel dress?

When I cut my eyes, and looked hard for a moment, I knew that girl. It was the girl from Prettyman Coburn! The bell-ringer girl!

It's too bad her mother wouldn't let her buy the Peach Melba dress. It looked good on her. Her hair is pastel to match the dress. And with all that twirling, she made the dress come alive.

But as *my* mama was folding *my* Peach Melba dress into a Millerton's shopping bag, *her* mama was forcing the other Peach Melba dress back on its hanger, and onto the dress rack.

Later, I heard Mama tell Daddy we'd be eating Goober's peanuts for dinner till September since they'd spent so much money on that stupid dress.

Daddy said, "I'll eat peanuts till I'm older than Methuselah if it means my Dawnie can look proper for her Stepping Up."

Sunday, May 30, 1954
Diary Book,

Shepherd's Way Baptist Church has to be the loudest congregation in all of Lee County. Services start off slow, but as Reverend Collier works up his sermon, the *amens* and *hallelujahs* can be heard all the way over in Norfolk, and they grow like the swell of dust that rises after sliding into third base.

This morning, Reverend Collier talked about integration. He even took out the New York newspaper Daddy had shown me, and read from it as part of his sermon. He rattled the paper, turned it into a fluttering fan to cool off his parishioners.

"This is the truth. Right here," he proclaimed. "In the *New York Times* from a week ago last Tuesday."

Seems everybody had read the same article Daddy had shown me. And for anyone who hadn't, Reverend Collier spelled it out for them. "Chief Justice Earl Warren from the Supreme Court says, 'Separate educational facilities are inherently unequal.'"

The *amens* started up. Reverend Collier flapped and fluttered the New York paper. "Says here that separating black children from others of similar age and qualifications because of their race" — ten more *amens* before the reverend could finish — "generates a feeling of inferiority as to their status in the community that may affect their hearts and minds in a way unlikely to be undone."

You would have thought Reverend Collier was announcing that the Shepherd's Way choir was getting new silk robes with gold trim.

"Glory be!" shouted Miss Eloise, our choir director.

"Hallelujah!" flung forward from somebody behind me.

"Amen!" rose on all sides.

When we got home, I asked Mama if I could please put on my Keds and go outside. She was so busy peeling potatoes that she shooed me off with a quick, "Go play, child."

Soon as I laced up my Keds, I was the one filled with:

Glory be!
Hallelujah!
Amen!

I ran to find Goober, who was perched under the tree mop, crunching on his peanuts.

Tuesday, June 1, 1954
Diary Book,

Why is everyone making such a big deal about the Stepping Up ceremony? We're not really stepping *up* to anyplace.

Even though we're going from sixth grade to

seventh grade, we're staying at Bethune, like all the other colored kids in Hadley. All we're doing is stepping *over* from the elementary "division"—the side of the building that faces Monroe Street—to the middle school "division"—the wing that lines Crossland Avenue.

We're stepping *over* to more chewed pencils, more stinky bathrooms, more books with missing pages. And did I mention that Bethune does not have a library?

Wednesday, June 2, 1954
Diary Book.

Today, along with Yolanda and Roger, I took the test Mr. Calhoun described to us last week.

It started off easy enough, and I was even humming "When the Saints Go Marching In" just to stay awake.

I wrote, checked off boxes, and filled in blanks without even sweating. But then something strange happened. Not strange like a noise or a bird flying in the window. But strange inside me.

Suddenly, I knew the answers, but I *didn't* know the answers, too.

The test was easy as cake, but it started to feel hard somehow.

It was when my mind began to stray that this happened. I looked around at the other kids in the room and wondered, *What is this test really for?* That's when I struggled with the answers.

One question I will never forget: *Provide a word beginning with the letter* M *that defines a powerful force that propels in a tumultuous fashion.*

I read it over and over again.

I broke it down.

. . . a powerful force . . . that propels . . .

Since the clock on the wall is broke, I couldn't tell how much longer we had left to finish the test. I don't know what the word *tumultuous* means. I didn't want to just write anything, because if I'd wanted to change my mind I wouldn't have been able to erase my answer — my chewed-up pencil had a bitten-off eraser. Why hadn't I brought my new red pencil from Goober?

Mr. Calhoun gave us a time warning. "Two more minutes."

And for the first time ever, I started to sweat a test!

. . . beginning with the letter M *. . . a powerful force that propels . . .*

I wanted to chew hard on some of that

Wrigley's gum that was stuck in a wad under my desk.

Finally, with Mr. Calhoun's "One more minute" warning, I wrote: "MY pogo stick."

Thursday, June 3, 1954
Diary Book,

I've been trying not to think about the Stepping Up ceremony, but it's now a week away, and I guess I should get my speech together. I don't even have a title for the speech, or any idea about what I should say.

I don't believe in the boogeyman, but I *do* believe in the Panic Monster—a big scary thing that scoops you up and does the *shaboodle-shake* all over your insides.

Mama calls this *nerves.* I call it a puddle under my arms, a dry throat, and teeth set to chatter.

The Panic Monster has got me in his claws right now, and won't let go.

Friday, June 4, 1954
Before Bed
Diary Book,

Mama came into my room with the dress from Millerton's on a hanger. She wanted me to try that thing on. The dress rustled under the paper Mama had draped over it. By punching a hole through it with the hanger, the dress stayed covered from its shoulders to its hem. I tried to pretend I'd fallen asleep, but Mama wasn't having it.

"That is the fakest snore I will ever live to hear," she said.

I giggled. "Can I try it on tomorrow?"

Mama considered me for a moment. She peeled back the dress's paper drape. "Well, I suppose we should let the creases fall out from the dress before trying it on," she said.

I went back to making phony snore sounds.

Kaaaa . . . shooooo . . . Kaaaa . . . shoooo . . .

That left Mama giggling, too.

Saturday, June 5, 1954
Diary Book,

Daddy loves baseball as much as me. Today he showed me how to choke up on the bat, to grip it firm at its base so my swing packs more power.

"Then *meet* the ball," Daddy instructed. "Make friends with the ball as the pitch approaches you. No matter how fast it comes, say, 'Hey, ball, it's me and you, baby.' Then swing at it. And when you swing, be *intentional*," Daddy said. "Go at it fully — mean to do what you mean to do."

Daddy and I practiced in our backyard for near to an hour. When the sun got too hot, Mama brought us lemonade.

"Let the child rest," she told Daddy. "She needs to come inside and work on her speech for the Stepping Up."

Mama had that Peach Melba thing in her hand. She'd removed the paper covering completely. "Come, Dawnie," she coaxed. "You need to try this on."

"I've been playing, Mama. I sure wouldn't want to get dirt or grass stains on that pretty dress."

That worked better than fake snores. Mama didn't even answer. She turned back toward the house, holding the dress away from her.

Daddy must have seen the relief come to my eyes. "Are you *ever* going to try it on?" he asked.

"I gotta write my speech" was my answer.

"I suppose the dress won't really matter unless your speech is ready," he said. Then he told me to think of the speech as *meeting* a baseball with a bat. "It's you and your message, coming together," he said. "Keep it simple."

I wish it *was* simple. I have not written a single word of that blanged speech!

So, right here, right now, I'll start.

Hey, speech. It's you and me. Simple, right?

How come, then, I can't think of something *simple* to say?

Sunday, June 6, 1954
Diary Book,

I thought maybe if I wrote down some of the reasons why I don't want to give the Stepping Up speech, it'll help me get to reasons why I might *like* to give it, and then maybe I'll actually think of what to say for the speech.

Reasons I don't want to give the Stepping Up speech:

1. I don't want to wear the Peach Melba dress.
2. I don't want to wear the hard black shiny shoes.
3. Even though I have the gift of gab, it doesn't work for giving speeches.
4. *Stepping over* doesn't deserve a speech.

Monday, June 7, 1954

Dear Mr. Jackie Robinson,

I have not written one single word for my Stepping Up speech. The ceremony is four days away.

Has this ever happened to you? Have you ever had to give a speech, and had no idea what you're gonna say? That's what's happening to me right now.
Speechless,
Dawnie Rae Johnson

Tuesday, June 8, 1954
Diary Book,

I've had my pogo stick for as long as I can remember. It's rusty and rickety, and it squeaks, but it still works.

I slammed hard on its pedals today, hoping a bunch of pogo jumping would bring on some good ideas for my speech.

Not one speech-y thought came. Punching the pavement with my pogo sure felt good, though.

That pogo's spring is on its last leg, but it keeps going. My own legs are getting stronger every time I pump.

Thursday, June 10, 1954
Late night
Diary Book,

The Panic Monster doesn't ever sleep, no, no, no.

He gets into his rhythm, and *works*. Tonight he's going double-time.

Shaboodle-shake-shake. Shaboodle-shake-shake.

I'm as rattly as a loose screw in a can.

Tomorrow is the Stepping Up ceremony.

The only speech I know is the Pledge of Allegiance.

Panic Monster, have mercy!

Friday, June 11, 1954
Diary Book,

It's just after the in-between. I've been up most of the night. Now the sun is showing off the very top of her head.

Morning soon.

Still no speech.

Shaboodle-shake-shake. Shaboodle-shake-shake.

Later

Today was the Stepping Up ceremony, and in all my twelve years of life, I have never *stepped* like that.

Getting ready to go to Bethune was the worst part.

The Peach Melba dress didn't fit me right. When I came out of my bedroom, Mama and Daddy were like two hovering chickens, peck, peck, pecking.

The Panic Monster flaring up alongside my parents didn't help matters. I was sweating more than a cold pitcher of iced tea set out on a hundred-degree day.

"The dress is too small," I said.

I turned around so they could both see that the dress's zipper would only go halfway.

"Square your shoulders, Dawnie," Daddy said. "That'll help."

Who knows how a father figures out stuff like that? But Daddy was partly right. When I stood straight-straight, with my shoulders pressed back and my neck lifted, the dress seemed to fit better.

"We can't take any chances," Mama said, scurrying off to get her sewing basket. "Stay just like that, Dawnie."

I didn't move. I held my breath, even.

Mama came quick with a needle and peach-colored thread. She started stitching from the place where the waist of the dress joins the body part of the dress—Mama sewed me in! The only thing closer was my skin.

I have other dresses I could have worn, but they're homemade and plain, and I knew Mama and Daddy were set on me wearing the dress from Millerton's. Besides, I don't dare challenge Daddy and Mama, not ever. So I let Mama do her needle-and-thread busywork up the length of my back.

When Mama bit off the final tail of thread, I still had my shoulders fixed, and my neck stretched as straight as my pogo stick.

It got worse. Mama wiped down my new shoes with Vaseline to make them even shinier. Isn't patent leather shiny enough?

My face came next. Same Vaseline. Same high shine on my forehead, cheeks, and nose. Then there was the talcum powder. "To keep you dry," Mama explained.

I coughed and coughed as Mama doused me with that thick talcum. The powder helped dry my sweat. But by the time we left, I was a ginger-snap cookie, decorated with powdered sugar, sewn up in a Peach Melba dress.

"Pretty Dawnie," Goober said, clapping. "Want a peanut, pretty Dawnie?"

I reached for a peanut. "Thanks, Goob."

But Mama was quicker than me. She snatched that peanut faster than a hen grabs at a kernel of corn. "No eating before you're about to give a speech. It weakens the voice, dulls the smile."

We walked to Bethune, like always. On our way, we met up with Yolanda and her ma and daddy. "You look good in that dress, Dawnie," Yolanda said. "But you're walking funny."

I didn't answer. Between the talcum still rising off me and my Peach Melba trap, I could hardly breathe.

The whole school — all four hundred and seventy-two students and their families — filled every corner of Bethune's gymnasium. Night crawlers in a can had more room than we did, all squeezed together in that hot, cramped place.

There were three chairs on the stage, where me, Yolanda, and Roger were meant to sit before delivering our remarks.

Roger and Yolanda settled into their chairs right away. I didn't dare sit. One bad move in that dress, and Peach Melba would be done for.

"I'll just stand," I told Mr. Calhoun.

"Suit yourself, Dawnie."

Roger spoke first, then Yolanda. They each said short thank-yous to their families and teachers, and talked about how glad they were to be "stepping up" to seventh grade.

Alls I could think about was the Pledge of Allegiance and the Peach Melba dress that was now choking me. The talcum powder wasn't doing its job. (The Panic Monster has a way of killing anything that's even the least bit helpful.)

I was so overcome with terror that I couldn't

even remember the Pledge of Allegiance. The wrong words kept filling me up.

I pledge allegiance to perspiration . . .

Then came the Panic Monster for the tenth time today, his sharp claws lifting me from the puddly place under my arms. His loud-as-thunder *shaboodle-shake* rattling inside my head.

Mr. Calhoun announced that I was the sixth grader with the best grades. That throughout my time at Bethune, I showed "very bright promise," and that I had brought honor to Mary McLeod Bethune's legacy.

I made my way to the very front of the stage, still not knowing what I would say.

I pledge allegiance to perspiration . . .

Shaboodle-shake-shake-shake!

Our school has no microphones or fancy equipment for speaking, so it was just me and all those people.

Shaboodle-shake-shake-shake!

Then me and all those people sucked in a loud breath when my too-tight dress busted its seams.

Mama's sewing stayed put in the back by the zipper, but the dress had split open on each side! Thank goodness for my undershirt. At least I had no skin showing! But the dress was no-doubt torn.

Not only did I step *up* at today's ceremony, I also stepped *over* to the place on the stage where nobody could see the rips in my dress. Then, quick as those Vaseline-y shoes would take me, I stepped *off* that stage and into a far corner.

Mr. Calhoun didn't try to coax me back with the other speakers. He just left me to my spot. He came to the front of the stage and started applauding loudly. Everybody joined him, including me. "Thank you, Roger, Yolanda, and Dawnie," he said enthusiastically.

And there it was, as it's been for weeks. No speech.

Peach Melba from Millerton's had saved me.

The Panic Monster started to let go. *Shaboodleshake* slowed its rhythm. At least I could breathe regular again.

As the top student in sixth grade, I got a copy of the Webster's Dictionary, donated by a local chapter of the Delta Sigma Thetas. The dictionary is used, but it's new to me, and in very good condition.

I pressed the dictionary under one arm to cover the open place showing my undershirt, and kept my free arm pinned to my other side to conceal the rip there.

Afterward, for a special treat, Daddy took me, Mama, and Goober to the Woolworth's food counter.

There is no colored section at Woolworth's. That place is "Whites Only" all over. We can order our food and leave, but we can't sit and eat with the white customers. We can't even come in the front door. There's a back entrance for Negroes.

When the waitress asked what we each wanted, Daddy gave the order.

We don't have special treats from Woolworth's often, but when we do, I usually get an egg cream. But, Daddy said, "For this occasion, Dawnie gets a banana *split*."

As soon as we got home, Mama took a seam ripper to the back of the dress, and released me. I don't know why she bothered to put the dress back on its hanger. I will never wear Peach Melba again.

Saturday, June 12, 1954
Diary Book,

Our family now owns two big books.

The King James Bible (Old Testament) and the Webster's Dictionary, also old. Even though the dictionary is used, it has all its pages as far as I can tell.

Daddy insists that I keep the dictionary in my room. "Smart children need books around them," he says. Man, is that book big.

How many words can there be in the world?

Tonight I read the article from the New York newspaper a second time. I looked up two words in my dictionary — *segregation* and *integration*.

Segregation: The state or condition of being separated.

Integration: The act or interest of combining.

If I wrote my own dictionary, I would call it *The Dictionary of Dawnie.*

Here are *my* definitions:

Segregation: Negro kids go to Bethune. White kids go to Prettyman Coburn. Colored people can't try on clothes or shoes they want to buy to see if they fit. We can *pay* for the clothes and shoes, but once we leave the store, we own the stuff whether it fits or not. Negroes can be hungrier than hungry, but we can't sit down at the food counter to eat at Woolworth's. We can be thirstier than sand in the desert, but we can't drink water from a fountain if that fountain's wearing a sign that says "Whites Only."

The same is true for swimming pools,

restaurants, and the Hadley Motor Hotel. They're all segregated.

Here is one more definition of *segregation* from *The Dictionary of Dawnie*:

Segregation: Stupid.
Integration: Pie-in-the-sky.

Sunday, June 13, 1954
Diary Book,

After church today, a strange lady came to our house. She had two men with her. I know most folks in Hadley, and most folks know me and my family. But I had never seen the likes of these people. The men were Negroes, but the lady was white. I could tell by the looks of them they were not from around here.

I have never in all my whole life seen a white person come into our house with so much ease! She had a weird way of talking, too. Or, maybe I should say *tawlking*. Every other word out of her mouth had a saw behind it. She asked Daddy if it was okay that she'd parked their *caw* in our driveway. And she didn't *tawlk* about her ideas — she was full of *idears*.

Even her clothes were not right. I'm smart for book learning, but I am no expert on girly fashion-y stuff. I do know, though, that wearing a black dress in the middle of the afternoon is what people do only for funerals. And I have never seen lipstick that dark on a real live person.

The Negro men wore suits, but the suit jackets had wide lapels and cuffed pants. Definitely not something I've ever seen in Hadley.

The not-from-around-here people spent near to a whole hour sitting in our living room. Drinking lemonade from our glasses, and *tawlking, tawlking, tawlking* to Mama and Daddy about their *idears*.

I was outside near an open window, so I caught snatches of what they were saying. I heard something about my Stepping Up speech.

Goober must have sensed something weird, too. He was very restless. He kept snatching my pogo stick and trying to slam his feet on it, and singing and screeching, "Dawnie can fly! Dawnie can fly!"

Finally, the people left. On the porch, Mama and Daddy shook their hands, even.

The white lady in the black dress gave Mama a hug! Right outside where everybody could see.

Goober and I were in the side yard. I'd given up my pogo stick to Goober. It was the only way to keep him quiet. We watched the not-from-around-here people drive away in their *caw.*

As soon as they were out of sight, I raced inside. "Did somebody die?"

Saturday, June 19, 1954
Diary Book,

Here's a secret I'm embarrassed to admit out loud, because it seems like a pie-in-the-sky wish that can't ever come true.

When I grow up, I want to be a doctor. I want people to call me "Dr. Dawnie Rae Johnson."

Other than studying hard, I'm not real sure on how I could get to become a doctor. I *do* know that I would have to first learn enough to be smart enough to somehow go to college, then doctor school.

What I *don't* know is how you get the learning you need that puts you *into* college so you can go to doctor school after that.

What I also *do* know is that whatever books and supplies a kid needs to learn the stuff to go to college, and then to doctor school, are not at Bethune. And what I also *don't* know is anyone who's ever gone to college.

That's why Dr. Dawnie Rae Johnson is as far away as Mars.

Tuesday, June 22, 1954
Diary Book,

Daddy brought me a present — a new Jackie Robinson baseball card! I have now read the stats on the card at least a hundred times. I'm tucking the card in my diary's safe gutter to mark today's date as the day the card got to be mine. The stuff about Jackie is sure nifty. Here are some Jackie facts:

* Jack Roosevelt "Jackie" Robinson

* Major League Baseball Debut: April 15, 1947, for the Brooklyn Dodgers

* Received the Major League Baseball Rookie of the Year Award in 1947

* The first Negro player to win the National League Most Valuable Player Award in 1949

* Bats: Right

* Throws: Right

I want to add one more fact about Jackie:

* Bravest player on the field.

Saturday, June 26, 1954
Diary Book,

Today I told Yolanda about my dream of being a doctor. Why in the world did I do that? I might as well have been telling her that hogs can dance the Hokey Pokey.

Yolanda laughed so hard.

She asked me, "Have you ever seen a colored doctor in Hadley?"

Well, no, I have never seen a colored doctor. Or a colored nurse, either. I've seen plenty of colored teachers and preachers, but no Negroes working in medicine.

Before I could answer, Yolanda told me, "My pa says there are only colored doctors in places like New York City, and not many of them."

What I didn't tell Yolanda was that I saw a colored lawyer once—I actually saw three colored lawyers.

I didn't see them for real, in person, walking around and talking. I saw their picture in the New York paper, along with the article about integration. I have un-pasted and re-pasted the picture part of that article here. The words under the picture say:

LEADERS IN SEGREGATION FIGHT: *Lawyers who led battle before U. S. Supreme Court for abolition of segregation in public schools congratulate one another as they leave court after announcement of decision. Left to right: George E. C. Hayes, Thurgood Marshall and James M. Nabrit.*

Those lawyers are sure smiling. They look real happy.

If there are Negro lawyers, there must be colored doctors and nurses, too.

Tuesday, June 29, 1954
Diary Book.

I just *had* to write two letters today, one to Jackie Robinson, and one to some other people I probably won't ever meet, but who I admire.

LETTER NUMBER 1

Dear Mr. Jackie Robinson,

My friend Yolanda squashed my dream of becoming a doctor before the dream even had a chance to grow. Her words hit me hard. Real hard.

Mr. Jackie Robinson, what did your best friend say when you told him you wanted to play baseball in the major leagues? Did he laugh hard and ask, "Have you ever seen a colored baseball player in the major leagues?"

I bet you're laughing now.

Signed,
Wanting to be Dr. Dawnie Rae Johnson

LETTER NUMBER 2

Dear George E. C. Hayes, Thurgood Marshall, and James M. Nabrit,

If you've ever seen a heel stomping on a wildflower, that's what it was like when I told my best friend that I wanted to be a doctor. Yolanda just smushed my wish. It hurt when she did that.

Dear lawyers, now that I have seen your picture and read about you, I know what's possible. But I have to ask—What did your friends say when you said you were going to be a lawyer? Did they smush your dream? Did it hurt?

51

Now that you've shown them what having a dream can mean, are they smiling as much as you are in that New York newspaper photograph?

Sunday, July 4, 1954
Diary Book,

Everybody and their brother comes to Linden Park for a picnic on the Fourth of July.

I don't know who decided to call Linden a *park*. The *park* is really just the back lot of Clem Linden's Barbershop, a place rusty cars and dandelions call home. It's home to us, too, one of the places in Hadley where white people won't go. We can be free to do whatever we want, how we want. Clem's got a small patch of collards growing next to his tomato plants, and a mess of pole beans coming out of the land like the legs of a giant.

Reverend Collier and his wife showed up at the same time we did. The reverend has the biggest car in all of Lee County. It's a Pontiac, with fenders so shiny, you can look into them and clean the corn kernels from your teeth.

Somebody had already set up tables of food. There were heaps of coleslaw and mac-and-cheese. And I had to wonder if there was a chicken left alive within twenty miles of Hadley. The tables were covered with drumsticks and thighs.

Yolanda's pa and Daddy played horseshoes with Clem Linden and Reverend Collier. All they talked about was this integration business.

Daddy said, "It's about time. But this is not going to be an easy fight."

Yolanda's pa said, "If integration means whites and blacks are supposed to go to school together, white children can come to Bethune. Let *us* teach *them* a thing or two. Let *us* show *them* how the other half lives."

Clem was quick to point out, "They're going to make our lives miserable. White folks can't stand knowing we're getting something they have. I'm not throwing my kids into that hornets' nest. My children are staying at Bethune."

The reverend said, "This is a time of hope for our children. The best way to make that hope into something real is to rise and meet it. "

Soon it seemed everybody was discussing integration. If collards could talk, they would have been debating with Clem's tomatoes.

I was sick of it all. I'm glad I'd brought my baseball bat. I was able to rustle a game together.

Reverend Collier volunteered to be the ump.

Freddy Melvin was the pitcher. Freddy's got

more hot air than a wind balloon with a basket underneath it. He makes my gift of gab sound like mumbling.

I was the first batter up. Freddy Melvin shouted, "Hey, grandma, you ready to play ball?"

"Just pitch it, will you?" I said.

Freddy pitched underhand, slowly. He was treating me like a girl player. When the ball loped at me, I caught it, didn't even try to swing.

I walked the ball back to Freddy. "Pitch it regular," I told him. "I'm ready to bat — and to run."

"Don't you need a cane for runnin', little old lady?" Freddy said.

Freddy knew I could bat the pants off anybody. He was just wisecracking.

His next pitch came fast, overhand.

Yeah, Freddy can call me "grandma" all he wants. But this granny hit a triple.

"Here's your ball back, gramps!" I called to Freddy. "I hear there's a sale on canes down at Millerton's. You might want to get one," I hollered from third base.

Roger Wilkes was up next. If I'm grandma and Freddy's gramps, Roger's great-grandpa. He moves slower than slow, and can't bat worth a dime. "Bring me home, Roger!" I yelled.

I sure wish Freddy had pitched Roger a slowpoke-y underhand girly pitch. Roger's the one who needed it, not me.

Freddy was making it worse by winding up his arm to show Roger he meant business. The pitch came — *shwoop!* Roger jumped back, out of its way.

"Strike one!" called Reverend Collier.

Freddy's next pitch was faster than the first. It tore past Roger.

"Strike two!"

"I wanna go home, Roger! Home, you hear?" I shouted.

Roger adjusted his eyeglasses. "Home, Dawnie." He nodded.

Schwooooop! Freddy's third pitch was a smear of white.

Roger leaned in, and managed a good hit!

He worked his way to first base.

I hauled it home.

Freddy came at me with the ball, trying to get me out before my feet landed on the base. But I was too fast for gramps.

"Safe!" called Reverend Collier.

It was sure true. Today in Linden Park, I was as safe as could be.

Man, that baserunning felt good. As summer's heat hugged its warmth around me, integration flew far out of my mind.

Sunset's light had called every mosquito in Hadley, inviting them to leave a dotty map on my arms and legs.

Then came dusk. And fireworks dancing in the night sky.

Saturday, July 10, 1954
Diary Book,

Today was Goober's ninth birthday, and my turn to give him a special gift. I decided to take Goober to Ruttledge Street, where Mr. Albert sells bags of roasted peanuts with salt. He peddles peanuts from a cart, along with squash, peaches, rhubarb, and cukes. Mr. Albert is a member at Shepherd's Way Baptist Church, and he told me to bring Goober by for the peanuts, for free, since it's his birthday.

Goober ate the peanuts fast. There was a film of salt left at the corners of his lips when he was done. He licked at the salt. "I'm thirsty," he said.

Every Negro child in Lee County knows that when you're thirsty, and there's no colored drinking fountain, you drink your own spit till you get home.

But Goober, he doesn't know nothing about colored water fountains, or those marked "Whites Only."

He kept whining, "I'm thirsty. I'm thirsty." And before I could stop him, he was running fast to get water from a "Whites Only" fountain.

I know a water fountain doesn't care who drinks its water. But white people care. They really care.

Goober got to the "Whites Only" fountain, and started slurping the water. Then he dipped his face down into the basin to cool off! I have never been more scared for Goober than when I saw three white boys coming up on him from behind. I knew those kids. They were the Hatch brothers, Bobby, Cecil, and Jeb. Their daddy owns Hatch Hardware.

"Goober, get back!" I shouted.

Goober startled, then lifted his face, which was glistening from the water.

The boys had circled around Goober, who was offering them a drink from the fountain.

Bobby, the oldest Hatch brother, is my same

age, but much taller. He said, "Well, if it ain't a Negro retard!"

My heart was a fast pitch inside my chest, making its way to my throat.

The Panic Monster had sharpened his claws, and did they ever pinch!

"My brother can't read good," I managed to say. "He was thirsty. He made a mistake. But we're leaving now."

Jeb Hatch said, "Look, is that a colored girl, or a colored boy? Can't tell by the dungarees."

Mr. Albert had left his cart and come over. He looked just as scared as I felt inside. "Goober, Dawnie, get on now. Go home, you hear me?"

But Goober said, "Want some water, Mr. Albert?"

I didn't want to holler at Goober. That would scare him. He didn't know what was happening.

Mr. Albert folded one arm around Goober and one around me and backed us away slowly.

"Get outta here, and take that Negro retard with you!" Cecil called.

All three Hatch boys started to chant. "Negro retard! Negro retard!"

Then came sticks.

And spitting, too.

Daddy and Mama have told us to always tell them when we have a run-in with white folks. But telling about run-ins always leads to more trouble somehow.

It is late night as I write this. Goober has been rocking in his sleep.

And singing very quietly, *"Happy birthday to me,"* as he dreams.

And whispering "Negro retard" into his pillow.

Monday, July 12, 1954
Diary Book,

It's the in-between. Not night, not morning. I'm folded into my bedroom's tiny closet with a flashlight, writing.

It's hot as blazes in here, and the only good air is what's slicing through the crack of my partway open door. I've come to my closet because what I'm about to tell you feels supersecret. And, Mama has some kind of special power that lets her know when I'm awake, or when I've got my flashlight on under my covers. I don't want to beckon whatever that thing is in Mama.

Yolanda told me that same white lady and the two Negro men in city suits came to her house.

"Did they sit in your living room?" I asked.

Yolanda nodded.

"How long did they stay for?"

"My daddy showed them to the door soon after they started talking," she said.

I told Yolanda how the lady hugged Mama.

Yolanda's eyes went wide. "Hugged for real — like, touching each other?"

"For real," I said.

That's when Yolanda fished a crumpled sheet of paper from her pocket. It was a mimeograph copy of a flyer with lines for people to sign their names.

"This is what the two men and that lady gave my ma and daddy before they left."

I have the steadiest hand in Lee County, on account of how firm I can hold a baseball bat. But my hand, all on its own, has a little quiver to it right this minute. And I'm doing something I hate when others do it, especially at school — I'm chewing on the pencil Goober gave me.

The paper Yolanda showed me has Mama's and Daddy's signatures on it.

I am pasting it here, just to make sure it's real, and that this is not one of those dreams like when a Martian comes and takes you to someplace green.

Right off, I recognized Mama's curly signature and Daddy's blocky way of forming letters. They'd signed me up to attend Prettyman Coburn, come September!!

Later – Full Morning
Diary Book,

Is what I pasted during the in-between really here? Or is it part of a Martian dream?

I'm going to flip your thick pages back, one . . . two . . . three . . .

**NATIONAL ASSOCIATION FOR THE
ADVANCEMENT OF COLORED PEOPLE (NAACP)
TAPS TOP STUDENTS TO START
INTEGRATION PROCESS.**

Parental Consent Required.
Student Name: Dawn Rae Johnson

Grade as of September 8, 1954: 7

Parents:

Loretta Johnson
Curtis Johnson

Thursday, July 15, 1954
Diary Book,

Yolanda's no pogo-stick expert, but she's good at rhyming and singing. Today I jumped high and hard on my pogo, while Yolanda set my pumping to a song.

> *Pogo, pogo,*
> *Where do we go?*
> *To the clouds.*
> *To the sky.*
> *Jumping, pumping, way up high.*
> *Pogo, pogo,*
> *Where do we go?*
> *To the moon.*
> *To the stars.*
> *Take a pogo trip to Mars.*

Monday, July 19, 1954
Diary Book,

There was a small item in today's newspaper about the All-American Girls Baseball League. It looks like the owners of the AAGBBL will decide to suspend play for the 1955 season. Some of the players will keep touring around, but eventually the AAGBBL will call it quits. The paper said the crowds at the baseball parks, coming to see girls play, are drying up. How can that be? Who wouldn't want to see the best girl batters, pitchers, and base runners around?

Now I'll never get to play in the league. I hope Yolanda doesn't ask, "Have you ever seen a Negro player in the All-American Girls Baseball League?"

I was planning to be the first one.

Thursday, July 22, 1954
Diary Book,

Tonight for supper Mama served my favorite two foods — pulled pork and fried pickles. When I came to the table, Goober had set up his peanuts in the shape of a happy face, smiling at the center of us all.

Right off, I asked, "How come we get special food on a regular night?"

"We're celebrating," Mama said.

Mama and Daddy explained some of what Mr. Calhoun had told us, that the test I had taken at school with Yolanda and Roger had been issued by the Department of Education for the state of Virginia. They said that because of the test results, I'd been picked to attend Prettyman Coburn in September.

They told me the test was set up to be very hard so that even me and the other smart kids at Bethune couldn't pass it. If we all flunked, the Department of Education would have a reason to keep us out of Prettyman.

"I don't ever flunk," I said.

Mama nodded. "You three kids who took the test passed."

She told me I only missed one question. I knew the question Mama was talking about. She said, "They showed us your test." Mama looked pleased. "On one of the questions, the test asked to give a word that means a force that propels, and starts with the letter *M*. It said this force is tumultuous, like a storm."

I told Mama, "That question didn't say anything about a storm."

"Anyway," said Mama, "the correct answer was *maelstrom*."

I folded my arms. "What kind of word is *maelstrom* to give to a kid on a test?"

Mama said, "You did very well on the test, Dawnie. That's what matters most."

Daddy was smiling and shaking his head. He said, "'MY pogo stick' *does* start with the letter *M*."

He told me about the white lady in the black

dress and the colored men in big-collared suits who'd come to our house. They were from the NAACP, a group of people whose members work to get equal rights for Negroes.

"How come that lady was *tawlking* funny?" I wanted to know. "And how come she hugged you, Mama?"

Daddy answered with a question. "How come you weren't minding your business, Dawnie? That was a private meeting between grown-ups."

Goober had set a fried pickle spear onto his plate, and had made a pickle-shaped man with peanut arms and legs. "Funny *tawlking*. Grown-ups funny *tawlking*," he said.

I didn't dare mention the paper Yolanda had shown me. Daddy told me the lady was from New York, and that's how Northerners speak, and that there's nothing funny about people wanting to help you. Even white people.

"That lady's name was Cynthia Woods," Mama told me. "She was very kind, and was pleased that we agreed with the work she and the others from the NAACP are doing."

Mama and Daddy told me that I'd get a better education at Prettyman Coburn, and, they reminded me, Prettyman is a far walk from where we live, a whole two miles away. "But you have a right to attend the best school in this district," Daddy said, "no matter how far it is."

I guess that meant I had the right to walk on those clean Prettyman sidewalks. And the right to say good morning to those pretty, pointy Prettyman trees out front. And to play on that pretty Prettyman baseball diamond after school.

I'd walk a million miles for that.

Yolanda doesn't own a telephone, so I couldn't call to tell her about how happy I was that she and Roger and me were chosen to be Prettyman students.

With all this news, none of us had eaten. Mama said grace.

"Pass the pork," Daddy said.

"Pass me a pickle," I said.

Goober said, "Look at my peanut-pickle person, Dawnie. See my peanut-pickle person, on my plate?"

Mama doesn't ever let us play with food, but tonight she allowed Goober his fun. "Let's eat" was all she said.

Monday, July 26, 1954
Diary Book,

Tonight after supper I asked Mama and Daddy if we could buy a TV.

They both answered at the same time: *"No."*

"Televisions cost money," Mama said.

"Money we don't have," said Daddy.

I don't know much about money, except that when you have a nickel, you can buy five pretzel sticks from Woolworth's. When you have a penny, you can buy a sucking candy. When you have a dime, you can buy a root beer. Last Christmastime, I got a penny, two nickels, and even some dimes. I didn't spend none of that money. Since I've been old enough to hold a penny, I've been saving to buy a new pogo stick, an Ace Flyer.

I also know this: When you don't spend money on things like Peach Melba dresses that are too tight and shiny shoes you don't wear much, you have more money in your pocket for a TV.

We were sitting out on our porch watching Goober chase fireflies.

The radio was on. We were listening to a commentary about an upcoming game between the Dodgers and the Red Sox when the program was interrupted.

The man on the radio said, "U.S. senator Harry F. Byrd vows to stop integration in Virginia schools."

"Get the baseball commentary back on!" I insisted.

For the second time, Mama and Daddy spoke together: *"Shhhh!"*

The man on the radio was talking about school, and I did not want to hear it! It's summer, right? Can we please not think about school?

Even Goober agreed. He'd caught a firefly in a jar, and ran to show me.

"Baseball back on!" he sang. "Baseball back on!"

Wednesday, July 28, 1954
Diary Book,

Yolanda and I played our favorite game today. A game we call "Tell the Truth or Die Tryin'."

Yolanda always starts truth tellin' by making an X over her heart with her pointer finger. "Cross my heart, hope to die. Stick a needle in my eye. If I'm lyin', watch me cryin'. 'Cause I know I will be dyin'."

Then we press our foreheads together to see if either one of us has shed a "lyin' cryin' dyin'" tear, and to seal the truth between us.

Today Yolanda said she wouldn't be coming to Prettyman with me. Her parents don't believe in integration, especially her father. "My pa says why go to a place where you're not wanted."

I didn't believe Yolanda at first. She said, "Cross my heart, hope to die. Stick a needle in my eye. If I'm lyin', watch me cryin'. 'Cause I know I will be dyin'."

She had to be lyin'. This could not be true.

"Are you telling me a story, Yolanda Graves? 'Cause if you are, cut it out."

Yolanda shook her head. "I'm telling the truth, Dawnie, I swear."

Yolanda didn't need to cross her heart to show me she *wasn't* lying. Her down-in-the-mouth expression told me she was being real.

Then I remembered the paper Mama and Daddy had signed. I'd been so flabbergasted by seeing their names, that I'd forgotten to look to see if Yolanda's parents had signed the form, too. I guess they hadn't.

"Well, if *you're* not going to Prettyman, *I'm* not going, neither," I said.

But I didn't mean that, and Yolanda knew it, too.

"You gotta do it, Dawnie," she said. "How will

we ever know what it looks like inside that school if you don't go?"

"Roger Wilkes can tell us."

Yolanda said, "Roger Wilkes's glasses have more smudge on them than a windshield stuck with mosquitoes. I'm surprised he can see his own feet."

Yolanda wouldn't look at me. "Besides," she said quietly, "Roger's not going to Prettyman, either. His daddy and ma wouldn't even open the door for those NAACP people."

"So it's just me?" I asked.

Yolanda kicked at the gravel under her feet. She nodded. "It's just *you* going to Prettyman, Dawnie."

Just me?

If a balloon could feel what it was like to be sat on at a birthday party, it would know what I felt right then — *pop!*

Saturday, July 31, 1954
Diary Book,

This weekend, Reverend Collier is hosting folks from Calvary, a visiting congregation from Reston. To welcome them, we held a church-wide picnic at Orem's Pasture.

I don't know who does the naming of places in Hadley. Orem's Pasture isn't really a *pasture*, like where cows gather. Orem's is a raggedy patch of crabgrass that separates Ivoryton from Crow's Nest. It is the closest we come to the white part of town. The grass is more brown than green, but the *pasture* is wide, and offers plenty of open space, and is closed in by a chain-link fence.

Seeing as there were so many people needing to picnic, I guess Reverend Collier chose Orem's to give us all enough room for spreading our blankets.

There was a boy from Calvary who'd brought two baseballs, a bat, a bunch of mitts, and even an umpire's mask. I'd brought my bat, too. And my mitt.

The kid's name was Lonnie. He called together a baseball game soon after everyone from both congregations had gathered.

All the boys from Calvary came to the center of the pasture. So did the boys from Shepherd's Way. So did I.

Lonnie looked at me sidelong. "This ain't softy ball," he said. "It's a baseball game."

What Lonnie didn't know is that I can knock

the jelly out of any ball that comes at me, and that I'm no softy.

Freddy Melvin spoke up quick. "Let her play," he said.

Lonnie wasn't having it. "No girls."

Freddy made a sour face like he was being forced to eat okra. But he was faking. "We'll put up with her."

Fake sour face and all, Freddy wanted me on his team. "We can stick her in the outfield," he told Lonnie.

Now I was the one making a sour face. "The *outfield*?" I protested. Everybody in Hadley knows I'm a second baser, just like Jackie Robinson.

"You wanna play, or not?" Freddy asked.

"Yeah, I *wanna play*. But I *wanna play* where I *can* play, not dawdle with the butterflies."

"Dawnie, when it's time to bat, you'll play, 'kay?"

"Not *okay*," I huffed.

But Lonnie was already assigning his players and the game was starting.

It was Shepherd's Way against Calvary.

Roger was quick to join our team. Goober, too.

"They playin'?" Lonnie asked.

There's only one thing I hate about baseball—

losing. I couldn't tell Roger not to play, but I had some control over Goober.

Before I could think of a way of gently encouraging Goober *not* to play, Mama was at centerfield volunteering him.

"Goober can set up," she said, and she started helping Goober make bases from whatever was nearby.

Together Mama and Goober drove the nose of a pop bottle into the dirt to mark first base. Second base was a box top. Third, a snatch of tire rubber. Home plate was a sock Goober had found and stuffed with newspaper. This seemed to satisfy Goober's wanting to be on the Shepherd's Way team.

Mama, Daddy, Goober, the Reverend, and a whole mess of people from Shepherd's Way pulled their picnic blankets closer to the game. Yolanda was there, too. "Make it happen, Dawnie!" she shouted. "Show 'em you mean business, girl!"

The Calvary team was up first. That Lonnie kid, he sure knew his way around swinging a bat. He met Freddy's fastest pitch with a mean *crrrrack*, giving me some play way out in the pasture. I scooped the ball, hurled it. But by the time Roger stumbled over his feet, Lonnie was home free—and home-run happy.

When it was our turn up, Freddy let me bat first. Lonnie was pitching.

"Bring it home, Dawnie!" Daddy shouted. "Don't just swing. Use your noggin. Think, child. *Meet* the ball."

"Home, Dawnie!" Goober cheered.

I had a good grip on the bat. Hiked it high over my shoulder. I was ready. Feeling confident. Feeling fine.

When I surveyed the pasture, there was rattling coming from the fence. All three Hatches had shown up, and were watching from the spot closest to Ivoryton, where the fence separates Orem's Pasture from the road. They didn't dare pipe up or misbehave. There were only three of them, but lots more of us, including grown-ups. Just having the Hatches around bothered me, though. I tried my best to ignore them, but it was hard doin'.

It helped having Daddy coaching me from the sidelines.

"Chin up, Dawnie!"

Lonnie slammed in a pitch. Man sakes—there was fire on the stitches of his ball!

"Strike one!"

Lonnie craned his knee high up, brought the ball back — *flam!* That pitch was hotter than the last. It could have melted the fenders on Reverend Collier's Pontiac.

The two words every batter hates shot up from behind me: "Strike two!"

I released my bat for a moment. Did the thing that riles Mama most — spit in both my palms. "Choke the bat!" Daddy coached. "Choke it, Dawnie!"

Lonnie's teammates cheered him. "Put it down the middle, Lonnie-man! Show her this ain't no place for a girl."

Lonnie bombed me with his pitch. As slammin' as it was, I never lost sight of its power. I didn't hit the ball, I *laced* it — high and far, all the way to St. Peter's post at the pearly gates.

I put some smooth peanut butter on that jelly doughnut.

Flung my bat, and breaknecked like heck toward the pop bottle in the dirt — to first base.

It sure helps being big-legged. A box top never looked as good as when I was landing on its second-base square.

Soon that rubber tire patch was calling my name — third base!

Now *I* was bombing forward, blowing through puffed cheeks, working my way to the stuffed sock, to home base. My ball had soared so far and high that it took the Calvarys a good two minutes to get it back. Still, every baseball player knows you're not safe till you hear the ump make the call.

As I watched that stuffed sock get closer, I could hear Lonnie hollering to his outfielders, "Get the ball. She's near to home!"

Daddy must have kept Mama from fainting at what came next. I didn't just *slide* into home base, I *sliiiiiid* on my belly, mopping the land with the front of my shirt.

I'm not one for eating dirt, but dirt from *sliiiiiiding* into home base tastes sweeter than brown sugar. Never mind that it stung my eyes. I was nose-to-the-ground, smelling that musty sock, smelling home.

"Safe!" came the call.

I got to my feet, danced a happy kick-step. Brushed the brown sugar from my front.

Our game continued through the afternoon. I hit a double and two more homers.

Shepherd's Way beat Calvary, but only by a little.

It wasn't until the game was over that the

Hatch boys left. They'd hung tight to the fence, fingers laced to its chains, watching me play.

Sunday, August 1, 1954
Diary Book,

Calvary's minister, our guest speaker, delivered today's sermon. "The Lord doesn't take sides," he said. "But he does know good baseball when he sees it. Yesterday, the players from Shepherd's Way gave the Lord a front-row seat to some lively ball playing."

Wednesday, August 4, 1954
Diary Book,

Today was hotter than the hinges on the devil's front door. Daddy and Mama took me on a practice walk to Prettyman Coburn so that we could see how long it would take to get there from home, and to make sure I'm clear about the directions on foot. Mama and Daddy don't know anything about the shortcuts Yolanda and I have found, so we walked the main streets, the longest way to get there.

Two miles is no fun in the heat. I'd started out on my pogo stick, but took to hoisting it across my shoulders after just a short time. Goober noted the streets and avenues, calling out their names as we walked.

Mama and Daddy peppered me with rules about what to do and not do when I attend my new school.

Mama's rules were about being polite and not making trouble. Daddy was strict about safety.

All the rules started the same way:

"Always remember . . ." and

"Don't forget . . ." and

"Make sure you . . ."

"Always remember—you catch more flies with honey than with vinegar."

"Don't forget to smile."

"Make sure you greet your new teacher courteously."

Daddy gave a warning.

"Rule number one," he said, "keep your hands to yourself."

Even Goober had rules—polite ones and safety ones:

"Give nice people a peanut," he said. And, "Give mean people three peanuts."

Diary Book,

Goober's not allowed to come out of our fence without first asking me or Mama or Daddy. Today he wanted a pogo lesson, but we had to stay in our small front yard to do it, which is not enough room for jumping, and not enough concrete for pumping good on the pogo stick.

I tried showing Goober how to pogo on grass, but my pogo kept sticking in the dirt. This made Goober cry, then wail. "I want to fly like you, Dawnie!"

He kept saying it over and over, louder and louder. Screeching like he does when he's upset. Then he slammed the pogo stick hard on the grass, and cried more. I sat him down on our back steps until he calmed down.

"Let's play airplane," I said softly.

Goober spread his arms wide. He ran in zig-zags around our yard.

"Watch out for the other planes, Dawnie, okay?"

"Okay, Goober."

"Do you see the other planes flying, Dawnie? Do you see them flying?"

"Yes, Goober, I see them."

Monday, August 16, 1954
Diary Book,

Daddy brought home a new magazine today. It's called *Sports Illustrated*. A whole magazine about sports! Its pages were shiny, and felt so good touching up against the skin on my fingers as I turned them. And the pictures—I couldn't stop staring.

Wednesday, August 18, 1954
Diary Book,

Without asking me, Goober played with my pogo stick. I don't like him touching my things, but the worst part is that he left the pogo stick out in the rain. The stick is already rusty enough!

I'm mad as a hornet right now, and ready to attack Goober!!! That boy!! Somebody needs to leave *him* out in the rain so that *he* can rust. At least then, he'd be too stuck to mess with my stuff.

I wish I could send Goober back to the planet where boys like him come from!

Right now, if it were up to me, I'd put him on a rocket ship, set the destination dial to "Way Far Away," and send Goober flying off for forever. I HATE when he does stuff like this. HATE IT!!

If Mama and Daddy ever heard me say what

they call "the *H* word" — H-A-T-E — I'd be the one sent off on a rocket, and made to live on Jupiter.

Mama says that in God's eyes there is no hate. But what about MY eyes? What about MY eyes that have to look at my rusted pogo stick and be hornet-mad every time I see the brown, crusted metal on the pogo's spring?

What about MY eyes that have to see what happens when Goober acts up?

So yeah, *HATE* is a bad word. But when your brother leaves your favorite-est thing in the world out in the rain, you HATE him for it.

That's why a diary book is good. I can write the *H* word as much as I want. I can feel H-A-T-E, but not ever say it.

I HATE having a little brother like Goober!!

I HATE putting up with his baby-brother dumbness.

I HATE being the one who has to stick up for Goober so much.

And I HATE that God made Goober the way he is.

HATE! HATE! HATE!

And, here are some more *H* words — HA! HA! HA!

Mama and Daddy can't stop me from writing H-A-T-E!!

Saturday, August 21, 1954
Diary Book,

Instead of calling my pogo a pogo *stick*, I should call it a pogo *stuck*. More rust has set in. The spring is crusted and slow to give. Darn that Goober!

Sunday, August 22, 1954
Diary Book,

I think Reverend Collier is getting lazy. His sermons used to be about things like finding joy in the Lord's surprises. Now all Reverend Collier talks about is integration and fairness in education.

Can't he think of some new ideas?

Thursday, August 26, 1954
Diary Book,

Mama says grease heals. Today she slathered my pogo's spring with bacon grease left over from frying, and it worked. That bacon grease made the spring like new. So, I'm back to jumping on my pogo stick. It now smells like pork strips, but at least I can say, "Bye-bye, pogo *stuck*."

Monday, August 30, 1954
Diary Book.

Other than Daddy's truck, our radio is the most expensive thing we own. The voices coming out of that brown box give us all kinds of news. Mama and Daddy listen close most every night. My parents are very strict about what we tune into with our radio. We're only allowed to play Christian music. Comedy shows, or anything Daddy says is a time-waster, are not allowed.

Thank goodness Daddy listens to baseball games. Other than that, "The radio is for news," Daddy says.

Who wants to hear some man talking about boring newsy stuff? I'd rather listen to quiz shows like *Break the Bank*. But Daddy's not having it. So, unless there's a baseball game on, I only half listen.

But tonight, I listened all the way when Daddy turned up the volume. The radio commentator said, "Virginia governor Thomas B. Stanley has appointed a thirty-two-member all-white Commission on Public Education to examine the effects of the recent *Brown v. Board of Education* school integration ruling. The governor has charged this commission with studying how the *Brown* decision impacts schools in the state of Virginia. The findings of this study will help the governor plan a course of action. The commission is chaired by Senator Garland Gray of Sussex County. It has been named the Gray Commission."

I didn't fully understand all the talk about commissions and findings. But I did know that Daddy and Mama were pressed to our radio.

Friday, September 3, 1954
Diary Book,

Why does summer seem to disappear the minute we turn the page on our kitchen calendar from August to September? Just yesterday I was fanning the sheen from my face with a dish towel, and wetting the towel with cold water to press on my forehead.

This morning I was fishing in my dresser drawers for something with sleeves until morning's chill gave way to warmth. I miss summer already. Even bee stings and sweat-weather.

Saturday, September 4, 1954
Diary Book,

School starts in four days. Alls I can think about is me at Prettyman Coburn.

Me on that pretty baseball field.

Me inside a school with working clocks and toilets that flush.

Me in a *homeroom*.

Me with white kids.

Only me.

With white kids.

Only, only.

Me.

(The Panic Monster has been whispering to me lately. His growl has been low, but there's no mistaking *shaboodle-shake!*)

Monday, September 6, 1954
Diary Book,

Today, when I asked Mama why we celebrate Labor Day, she said, "To acknowledge those of us who work, to pause on behalf of laborers." But there was no pausing in our house today. It was like we were getting ready to meet the queen. Some kind of scrub bug has bitten Mama. She spent the day sweeping and wiping all over our house.

"Is somebody special coming?" I asked.

"*You're* special," Mama said. "And you're *going* to a new school."

I started to ask what me going to Prettyman

has to do with furniture polish and a broom, but I held my tongue. Somehow, to Mama's way of thinking, a clean house means a good first day of school.

Tuesday, September 7, 1954
Diary Book,

Mama's gone cuckoo bird! Yesterday it was cupboards and carpets. Now it's me. Tonight when I took a bath, Mama scrubbed me cleaner than clean. She washed from my eyebrows to my toe jam, then set my hair on hard plastic curlers. Those curlers have teeth on them, too. "For *gripping* your hair," Mama explained.

Now she expects me to get a good night's sleep on these teethy pink plastic things. Mama had given me a whole mess of curlers from her hair care kit, too many for my small head of hair. When I told her I didn't need the extra curlers, and to please put them back in her hair-care kit, she insisted that I keep a pile of the curlers on my nightstand. "They come loose and can fall out while you sleep," she told me. "Besides, curlers are like socks. They have a way of disappearing. Always good to have some handy."

While I was in the bathroom messing with the

curlers in my hair, trying to tie up my hard plastic teethy head in a scarf, Mama laid out clothes for my first day at Prettyman Coburn.

When I got back to my bedroom, there it was on a new hanger, dangling from the doorknob—the Peach Melba dress! Before I could protest, Mama explained, "I sewed a panel into each side to open up the bodice. It'll fit fine now."

The patent leather shoes were on the floor, side by side, at the foot of the dress. I'd taken to calling those shoes "the Vaselines." They had more grease on them than a petroleum factory.

The shoes fit, but even with ankle socks, they rub at the heel and on the tops of my feet, at the place where the buckle meets each of the straps. The worst part, though, is that Mama had made a hair bow to match the dress. That thing looked more like a *bone* than a bow. I would be going to Prettyman Coburn with Vaseline feet and a Peach Melba *bone* in my hair!

I didn't say a word—I *couldn't*. Partly because the only word flinging up inside my head was *ugly*, and partly because I didn't want to hurt Mama's feelings. She had worked hard on mending the dress, shining the shoes, and making the bow.

But what about my feelings? I don't give a nose hair what people think about me, but I also don't like to look stupid.

Later – the in-between

For the life of me, I can't sleep.

I've counted sheep, chickens, baseballs, the stars out my window, and the moans made by our pipes. I'm more excited than on Christmas Eve.

What shiny surprises will be waiting for me tomorrow?

Even with all my excitement, *shaboodle-shake* is rocking my bed — and my head.

Wednesday, September 8, 1954
Diary Book,

Last night I dreamed about the Panic Monster.

I woke up with a bad headache, from the curlers. When I took them out, their teeth had left marks on my forehead and at my ears. And my curled hair made me look like a muffin-head.

Mama secured the *bone* with four big bobby pins.

Then she and Daddy started in with repeating their lists of "Always remember . . ." and "Don't forget . . ." and "Make sure you . . ."

But before Mama or Daddy could get too deep into their rules, the phone rang. I answered it. I knew the voice right off. It was that white lady from the NAACP, asking to *tawlk* to Mama or Daddy.

I pushed the receiver at Mama. "Yes, hello, Cynthia," she said, with a smile in her voice. But soon Mama was frowning, and shaking her head, and saying, "I see . . . I see . . ."

When she hung up, she told Daddy and me that I would not be going to school today, that the Hadley school officials had put a stop to me attending Prettyman.

"When will I go?" I asked.

"The NAACP is working toward lifting the hold by noon today," Mama said.

But noon came and went. We waited for further news and instruction on what to do. The phone didn't ring once.

Finally, by three o'clock, Mama said, "Take off the dress and put it back on its hanger. Set the shoes in their box, and be careful with the bow."

I am the only kid in Lee County who got to skip the first day of school.

I now know what it's like to feel two ways at once — disappointed that I would not be admitted to school today, and relieved that I would not be admitted to school today.

As much as I didn't want to show up with muffin hair and a Peach Melba bow, I didn't want to *not* go to school at all.

Thursday, September 9, 1954
Diary Book,

Today was the same as yesterday. Waiting and wondering, and listening for the phone to ring. Goober has started school at Bethune. I don't like the ripped-up schoolbooks and raggedy pencils at Bethune, but I'm sure sick of sitting around while Mama scurries from the kitchen to the living room, wiping her hands on her apron, and telling me to keep clean.

Friday, September 10, 1954
Diary Book,

I've done the same routine several days this week—scrubbed in the tub, set my hair in curlers, woken up, put on the Peach Melba dress, and waited to hear if I'd be attending school or not.

Daddy says people who make the state laws are working to slow down integration. NAACP officials are meeting every day to determine if it's safe for me to go to Prettyman Coburn.

Today Daddy brought home three different newspapers and read, read, read. After supper, before Daddy left for work, he was pinned to the radio, listening close. I listened, too, hoping for some news. "Governor Stanley has called again for cool heads, calm, steady, and sound judgment," the man on the radio said. "Stanley started out in favor of integration, but has been swayed by the majority, and has, in recent weeks, been in support of segregationists.

"School board officials have threatened to close all Hadley public schools rather than integrate them."

I'm a trapped rabbit, eager to jump — right out of my skin!

Sunday, September 12, 1954
Diary Book,

Church was packed today.

Reverend Collier started his sermon by asking, "Who among us steps back in the face of a threat?"

He talked about what the school board was trying to do to keep schools separate.

The reverend ended his sermon by telling us, "Those who have faith always step forward."

Monday, September 13, 1954
Diary Book,

Back-to-school once meant back-to-boredom.

Back-to-books.

Back-to-Bethune.

Back-to-broken.

But today when I watched everybody except me go *back* to school for the second week, I wished I was also going *back* — to anything.

But I have been *held back* from school for dumb reasons.

Butterflies in a net have more freedom than me. At least they can breathe. I've been holding my breath for near to a week.

Thursday, September 16, 1954
Diary Book,

Sitting home. Waiting. Hair curled. Vaselines strapped on tight. Help!

Friday, September 17, 1954
Diary Book,

I am dying of Peach Melba *bone* disease. Could I at least wait in dungarees?

Sunday, September 19, 1954
Diary Book,

Well, I got my *back*-to-school wish after all. Turns out, I'm going *back* to Bethune tomorrow.

Back to bitten-up pencils and broken books. Mama and Daddy are sending me to Bethune for now, until people make up their minds about which school I'm going to for good.

Monday, September 20, 1954
Diary Book,

I don't know what's worse — no school, or old school. At least I can go *back* to wearing clothes that fit and hair that's nothing like a muffin.

By the way, in this year's classroom it's 11:20 all day long at Mary McLeod Bethune School. The books have yellow pages and are dog-eared. Today I stared and stared at my classroom's broken clock, and as yucky as chewed gum feels, I pressed both thumbs hard under my desk.

More than ever, I knew that Bethune doesn't have whatever it is I need to learn to go to college and doctor school.

It's like I wrote before. I have no idea *what* I need, but I know Bethune doesn't have it. That's why I want to go to Prettyman so badly. Even though

I have never set foot in that building, I have a hunch the kids inside are getting everything a girl needs to go to doctor school.

Wednesday, September 22, 1954
Diary Book,

Seems the only person happy to have me back at Bethune is Goober. "Dawnie's here," he said to everyone who would listen. I'm now in the middle school "division" at Bethune, and, boy, is it bad. It had rained all night, so the streets and sidewalks were red from the leaky bricks. A silt smell rose from the wet pavement. Double ugh!

There's something I hadn't noticed about Bethune before. It droops. Even when it's not raining, the building's shoulders slouch.

Kids who had been my friends in sixth grade were calling me uppity for wanting to attend Prettyman. Yolanda didn't even stick up for me.

When I asked to share her umbrella on the walk home, she said, "There's not enough room under here."

"Be that way," I said. "Rain suits me fine."

But not walking with my friend made something in me droop, too.

When I got home, my thumbs were red from pressing so hard under my desk.

Friday, September 24, 1954

Dear Mr. Jackie Robinson,
This whole thing feels like being stuck in the wrong dugout, waiting to bat. Wanting to run. Can we please just get this game started? I want to show Prettyman how Dawnie Rae can play.
From,
You-know-who

Saturday, September 25, 1954
Diary Book,

Mama does laundry for a living. She cleans, dries, irons, folds, and mends for families in Ivoryton. She's home most days, except on Saturday mornings when she delivers the clean linens and shirts to her customers.

Folks call Mama "Loretta the Laundress," mostly because she can remove stains better than anybody else, and could press the wrinkles from a raisin if she had to. Mama's iron works harder than a farm mule, and she's got her own special starch she's invented using potato water and lavender.

This afternoon when I helped Mama hang the wash, I asked, "Are we uppity?"

Mama had clothespins pressed between her lips, holding them while she secured a sheet onto the clothesline. She released the clothespins, one at a time, clipped each to a corner of the sheet, and stood back as the breeze billowed the sheet toward her. She said, "What kind of cockamamy question is that?"

I told her what the kids at Bethune were saying.

It's not often that Mama sucks her teeth, but today she did. "Dawnie," she said, "let me remind you of a simple truth my own mother taught me, and that I have repeated to you and Goober a thousand times — sticks and stones can break my bones, but names can never hurt me."

I've known that ditty ever since first grade, when Mama taught me the words to sing to that wisecracking Freddy Melvin, who once said I had beaver-tail feet.

"Sticks and stones" works most times, but today it didn't answer my question. If going to Prettyman Coburn will make me uppity, I need to know.

I definitely want good books and the secret for

going to doctor school, but I sure don't want to be uppity.

Sunday, September 26, 1954
Diary Book,

Daddy explained that the judges working in the federal courts have issued an order. Hadley has to give Negro students the option to attend the white school if we want to. Prettyman Coburn's got no choice — they *have* to let me enroll, or else they're gonna be in trouble with the law.

"They're kicking and screaming about it," Mama said. "But even crybabies can't stop what's right."

So, school integration is going forward. Tomorrow I report to Prettyman.

Tonight Daddy came and sat on the edge of my bed. With the curlers in my hair, I'd taken to sitting up at my headboard, hoping to fall asleep that way. It was easier than waking with tooth marks on my forehead.

Daddy held me gently by both my shoulders. He was looking at me squarely, so I knew to pay attention to what he was about to say.

He explained that the people from the NAACP

had advised that he and Mama not come to school with me, that having them there might cause trouble.

"What kind of trouble?" I asked.

"Dawnie, you may see a lot of people gathered outside of the school tomorrow. Not everyone is in favor of you attending Prettyman Coburn, and there might be some who protest. The NAACP officials feel it may be harder to protect you if we're there. Protesters may feel less threatened by one Negro child, versus all of us. If they see colored adults, they may get riled. This could cause them to want to retaliate."

I listened carefully. The skin at the tops of my ears went warm.

Daddy had more to say. "Dawnie, you were born with the gift of gab. But sometimes that gift is not to be shared. This is one of those times. If someone offends, lock your lip, child. Do you understand?"

I nodded.

Mama came into my room after tucking in Goober. She explained that she would walk Goober to Bethune, like always, and that Daddy would walk me part of the way to Prettyman, but needed to say good-bye on the corner of Waverly

Street and Vine Road. He would not come close to the school building.

Daddy's work shift had started earlier, and Mama would be picking up Goober from Bethune in the afternoons. So I would walk home from school by myself. "Just make sure you stay on the main streets," Daddy said. "And keep alert." I nodded again, twice this time, to show I understood.

After Daddy and Mama kissed me good night, I looked up two of Daddy's words in my dictionary.

Protest: An expression of disagreement or complaint.

Retaliate: To return like for like, often in an evil manner. To avenge, be out for blood, defend.

Now my whole ears were warm. My neck, too.

Monday, September 27, 1954
Diary Book.

If I live to be a hundred, and I'm stuck to a porch rocker with bad legs, three teeth, and a mind as rusty as a rained-on pogo stick, I will never forget today.

I hope I don't wear out my pencil in writing it all. But I can't help but tell everything. Just as it happened.

I was up and dressed while the moon still hung

above our house. Daddy had come home from his shift at Sutter's and was ready to take me to school when I came into our living room. Goober and Mama were up, too, eager for this day to start.

Mama had pressed my dress with a mighty will. The bow, too.

She'd packed my lunch in a molasses bucket, and wrapped the whole thing in the leftover fabric used to sew the panels into the sides of my dress. Even my lunch tin was ready to make a good impression.

It's one thing to *wear* a new dress and stiff shoes. *Walking* in them is a whole 'nother thing.

Daddy took my hand. We started out quietly. No talking, each embraced by the in-between. The sky was dressed in blue velvet. Stars decorated its cape. Our streetlights spread yellow pools onto the sidewalks.

Everything was still. Even the dew was asleep.

Daddy seemed to be thinking on something. His hand clenched mine. His jaw was tight. I was thinking, too. About Yolanda. About the New York lady with the black dress. About Goober. And most of all about Prettyman Coburn.

A raccoon stopped me and Daddy from

thinking too deeply. She peeked out from the fence post at the edge of Mrs. Thompson's tea-rose garden. That raccoon moved with a sure waddle, not the least bit bothered by us. She was so pretty. And special. Her black eye mask was decorated with two full rings of white fur, not just white brows like most raccoons.

"She's one-of-a-kind," Daddy said. "Like you, Dawnie."

Raccoons are plenty in these parts of Virginia, but there was no *plenty* about this raccoon. I've seen none other like her.

I named her right away, on account of how she moved. "Nice to meet you, Waddle."

Daddy and I slowed our walk. Then Daddy stopped. It was full-light then. Morning.

Night crickets had quit singing, but the bullfinches had joined up with the whip-poor-wills, and there was a contest between them for who could out-flute the other.

Daddy said, "This is where I say good-bye, Dawnie."

We were still four blocks from the school building. I wasn't scared to walk the rest by myself, just sorry to lose the warmth of Daddy's hand as he let go.

"Head on now, Dawnie," he said. "Show everybody how smart you are."

I pulled my lunch tin close. There was pride in Daddy's eyes, but he looked uncertain, too. He waited for me to reach Elber Street, one block closer to Prettyman, then he waved good-bye.

It was when I got to the corner that I saw parked police cars, with their siren lights flashing. There were people everywhere, gathered in a snarl, waiting. I saw boys and girls, and grown-ups — and the sheriff. They stood behind barricades.

When I read a sign that said MOTHERS AGAINST INTEGRATION, I knew they were waiting for me. Not once did I want to turn back. I had waited too long for this day. The clock on Prettyman's front said it was half past seven. School started at a quarter to eight. I was hard-pressed on how to get into school, but determined, too. I figured if I went around to the back entrance where Prettyman's field meets up with the gymnasium door, I could get inside that way. But my figuring wasn't fast enough. "There she is!" somebody shouted.

That's when the trouble started. The girl from Millerton's Department Store — the one with the peach-colored hair — came onto Prettyman's front steps with the school bell in her hand. She clanged the bell to signal the day's start. Something about the power of that bell called me forward. I was not going to be late on my first day.

I moved slowly along the street, then turned onto Prettyman's front walk, where the crowd pushed at the barricades. Even then I wasn't too scared because I was so eager to get inside.

The sheriff nodded toward one of the policemen, and four of them came up on all sides. They were carrying long guns! I wasn't sure if they were there to protect me or stop me. The police kept the people behind the barricades, pressing them back when they shoved to get at me. But even with all their force, the police could not keep those people quiet.

The Panic Monster came quick, *shook me hard*.

The protesters' mouths were twisted and angry. Their faces looked liked tightly crumpled balls of paper. And, oh, were their tongues ever sharp!

"There goes the monkey!" someone hollered.

"Kill that chiggeroo!" somebody else yelled.

The Panic Monster was holding so tightly. *Shaboodle-shake-shake-shake-shake.*

I tried to put my ears on the sound of the school bell, but it was hard not to hear the hatred in the people's voices. Bobby Hatch and his brothers had shoved to the front of the barricades. The very worst part of it—the part that frightened me most—was that they shouted mean things about Goober in front of all the other people.

"And she's got a brother, too. But he's more stupid than any monkey."

Shabooooodle-shaaaake-shaaaake-shaaaake-shaaaake.

In the crowd I saw a small girl, a child much littler than me. Her face looked kind. She was holding out a flower and a note. Her mama encouraged her to give me both of them. I smiled. So did she. But as she set the note in my hand, she spit on my new shoes. And the note wasn't a note at all. The little girl had drawn a picture. It was scribbly, but there was no mistaking its meaning. It was a picture of me on my pogo stick falling into a patch of pricker bushes. Underneath she'd written, "Scratch off the black."

Quietly, I just kept repeating what Mama had taught me. "Sticks and stones . . . Sticks and stones . . ."

I know the end of the rhyme says "names can never hurt you," but that's not true. Names *do* hurt. Hearing other kids yelling mean things was worse than a punch in the stomach. And it made me want to holler back, but I'd promised Mama and Daddy I wouldn't.

More than anything, I wished I'd brought my baseball bat with me. Not to use it, but just to have it nearby. Just to grip it as tight as I could. To give my clenched fists something to hold on to.

I was afraid my dress might rip. Not from not fitting me, but from holding in so much riled-up stuff at my insides.

When I finally got to Prettyman's front door, it looked so big. I knew that if I could just get inside, I'd be all right.

The policemen pressed in closer on each side of me as we made our way up the steps and into the building.

Prettyman sure lives up to its name. The wide hallways and tiled walls gleam under the morning sun that blesses them with her light. I was starting to see why the white part of town is called Ivoryton.

The policemen took me to the second floor, to the principal's office, where I sat and waited. And waited and sat. And had to use the bathroom, but didn't dare ask.

At least the Panic Monster had let up for now. I could see by the placard on his office door that the principal's name was Mr. Lloyd.

The phones rang all morning. Each time she answered, the school secretary spoke graciously. "Prettyman Coburn, may I help you?" And each time, she looked over the tops of her glasses at me.

I stayed very still. Watching the clock. Wondering when I'd be meeting my teacher. Nobody talked to me. My lunch tin rested on my lap. At two o'clock, the school bell started to ring from outside. Its clang was muted by the thick windows. When I looked out, the police cars and barricades were still there. But this time a grown-up was ringing the bell, not the girl from the morning.

Mr. Lloyd wouldn't speak to me, or look at me even. He explained to his secretary and the policemen that most parents had taken their children home soon after I'd come into the building, and that there weren't enough students at school for the teachers to teach. The bell was a signal to the teachers that the school day had ended. The principal pushed his chin in my direction. "This child's done for today," he told the policemen.

My insides started to churn. Back came the Panic Monster.

I didn't want to face those angry people with their signs and spitting. Thankfully, Mr. Lloyd told the policemen, "Take her out the back."

We left the building at the place where I'd hoped to enter, through a set of steps alongside the gymnasium that led to Prettyman's baseball field.

Maybe it was seeing those bases and that green-green grass that put a hankering on my feet. Maybe it was the sky so big above me. Maybe it was the bullfinches, free in the trees, and still singing. It didn't matter that home was two miles away. I took off my Vaselines. Held them tight by their straps. Hugged my lunch tin. Then I ran and ran and ran till I saw our house and Goober waiting for me inside the front fence. Mama was there, too, hanging laundry. She didn't see me coming until Goober called out, "Dawnie!"

Mama put both her arms around me and smoothed my rumpled hair. My muffin had lost its curl. My bow had flown off while I was whipping through the streets and avenues that led me home. Mama's hands smelled like her lavender laundry starch. Their gentleness was a sure comfort. She kissed me twice on my forehead, then by my ear. She whispered, "Dawnie, Dawnie, sweet potato pie."

Something inside me tumbled open, and I cried.

Evening

Pulled pork and fried pickles for supper. I tried, but couldn't eat none of it. My stomach was too tight. And queasy.

Goober sat with his chin rested on the table.

He rocked gently in his chair. He's been very quiet all evening. He hasn't looked at me much. His eyes have gone someplace else for now. He's locked himself off.

All through supper, Goober mostly watched the pickle person he'd put on my plate. Finally, softly, he said, "Eat, Dawnie."

"Not hungry, Goober," I said.

Tuesday, September 28, 1954
Diary Book,

The Panic Monster had a hold of me all night. He sure works hard, even when I'm sleeping.

Daddy had to wake me this morning. I'd slept past the in-between, past the clock, even.

"Dawnie, time for school," he said, rubbing slow circles on my back.

Mama was there, too, saying, "You don't have to shine, but you *do* have to rise."

There was light at my window. It startled me. Morning had snuck up on me.

I dressed quick. I could only stomach orange juice.

Mama had set out one of my church skirts, a simple blouse, and a cardigan. It was still more dressed up than if I were going to Bethune. At least Mama took pity on me, and let me wear a plain white headband, not a *bone*-y bow.

I hurried into my clothes. But the Vaselines—*uh-uh*. Mouse traps on my feet would have been more comfortable than those shoes. Mama and I agreed on my loafers, which I wear for everything except baseball.

Mama secured my knuckles around the handle of my molasses lunch tin, which she'd still dressed up in the Peach Melba fabric.

This morning my picture was in our town newspaper, the *Hadley Register*.

The headline said: SHE STANDS ALONE.

Daddy bought ten copies of the paper. He'd picked them up on his way home from the dairy supply, as newsstands were just opening.

I've clipped the article here:

The first steps toward school integration in Hadley began yesterday when one brave Negro girl entered Prettyman Coburn School. With courage and determination, the child faced hundreds of angry protesters who assembled in an effort to keep Prettyman Coburn segregated, and to prevent the child from enrolling.

Many parents have refused to let their children attend Prettyman Coburn School. By midmorning yesterday, several had come to the school to remove their children. In a statement, Spencer Lloyd, the principal at Prettyman Coburn, said, "Allowing Negroes to attend our school poses a hazard to the safety and wellbeing of our institution."

Local officials and members of the state legislature are in continued talks with Virginia governor Thomas B. Stanley about next steps in the process. Until further notice, school integration remains the law. Any Negro wishing to attend Prettyman Coburn School, or any white student wishing to attend Hadley's other public school, the Mary McLeod Bethune School, is free to do so under the laws set forth in the recent *Brown v. Board of Education* Supreme Court ruling banning segregation.

Even though the paper never printed my name, there were photographs of me going into Prettyman.

Looking at the newspaper pictures, I don't recognize myself. My hair is all muffin-y. My Vaselines are catching glints of light from every which way. And my face—*What is that eyes-looking-straight expression?*

Under my picture the caption says: "A Soldier for Justice."

Wednesday, September 29, 1954
Diary Book,

Today Daddy and I walked to school at a clip. We said our good-byes at the same corner, Waverly and Vine.

I saw the police cars up ahead, but very few other people. Seems the angriest folks had stayed home. It was quiet, too. Like a fever that flares one day, then cools the next. I sure didn't miss all that hollering, but I noticed right off there was no school bell. I did miss that.

I went around to the back of the building, where I'd left Prettyman yesterday, and got in that way. It was easy. The policemen didn't even see me. I came in on my own.

Walking two miles to school with Daddy is a long way, but today, moving through the corridors of Prettyman felt like a road that never ends.

Even though the floors in that school glisten — somebody sure has a good mop — there is no pretty scenery along Prettyman's halls.

This morning Mr. Lloyd gave me my class schedule and pointed me toward my homeroom. He wore the same pained expression as someone who was being forced to clean a skunk's den. He did not want to be doing this.

I walked with my eyes and feet forward.

Oh, did I get some ugly stares.

I know for sure that I look like a regular person. I have two arms and both my legs. I have one head on top of my neck. It's a round head like everybody else's. Even though my hair is still muffin-y from Mama's curlers, as far as I can tell, there are no trees or corn stalks growing out the top of my head.

And even though Mr. Lloyd was hard-pressed to direct me toward my homeroom, as far as I know, I do not smell like a skunk.

By most counts, I'm a normal girl. But with the way those kids were staring at me today, you'da thought I was a bearded lady at the Lee County Carnival. From morning to afternoon, there was all kinds of ogling at me in the hallways. And people got all quiet.

And stepped away to let me pass.

And whispered.

And watched.

And wondered if I was gonna bite them.

Balancing all my schoolbooks on my head would have been an easier weight to carry.

Just as heavy was meeting my homeroom teacher, Mrs. Taylor. She looks like a turtle with pearls, and glasses on a chain around her neck. Mrs. Taylor was not too happy to see me come into her classroom. Neither were the kids in that class. There was more silence than in a graveyard at midnight. I spotted Bobby Hatch right away. He stuck his tongue out at me when Mrs. Taylor had her back turned.

After that, I didn't look left, right, and especially not behind.

I kept my eyes up front, where I found my seat, and an uneasy peace.

The rest of the day was like walking through a field of fog. I somehow found all my classes, where silence and more staring met me.

When I got home from school, our small living room was filled with people — Reverend Collier, Mama, and of course, Goober. Those people from the NAACP were there, too. Daddy had left for work. They were all waiting for me. Their heads were down. They were holding hands, praying.

Soon as I saw everybody, I asked, "What'd I do?"

"We wanted to make sure you got here in one piece," said Mama.

One of the NAACP men said, "We're here to guide your transition into Prettyman."

"And to offer support to you and your family," said the NAACP lady.

Reverend Collier said, "While waiting for you to return from school, we were pausing for a prayer."

Goober spoke next. "Amen for Dawnie. No broken pieces on Dawnie."

I couldn't get my Keds on fast enough. I spent the rest of the afternoon in our yard, batting at the tree mop.

Goober sang, "Amen for Dawnie . . . Dawnie amen!"

Thursday, September 30, 1954
Diary Book.

Today I remembered what hard wanting is. Mrs. Taylor presented each of us with our class jobs for the school year. With the naming of each job came some kind of reaction.

It went like this:

Job: Line Monitor: The student who helps us line up.

Reaction: Two eager volunteers stood.

Job: Office Messenger: The person who takes notes to the school office.

Reaction: Boys mostly, saying, *"Me,* Mrs. Taylor."

Job: Morning Salutation: The student who reads the day's date in front of the class.

Reaction: Girls mostly, saying, *"Please,* Mrs. Taylor."

Job: Blackboard/Erasers: The kid who sponges the blackboard and claps dirty erasers.

Reaction: Silence. Let's not all jump at once. Not a *me* or *please* within fifty miles of Hadley.

Job: Bell Ringer: The one who rings the school bell mornings and afternoons.

Reaction: Every hand, including mine, up high. *Me* and *please* back so fast.

I didn't speak out like the other kids, but *me* and *please* were fighting each other all over my insides.

Mrs. Taylor explained that Melanie, the girl whose job it was to ring the school bell, would no longer be attending Prettyman. Her parents have sent her to a private school.

Later I overheard another girl tell her friend that Melanie's parents did not want their daughter going to school with a colored child, so they took her out.

Mrs. Taylor told us that Bell Ringer is a popular role among students, and requires what she said is "a level of responsibility."

I listened carefully when she explained that each year a student from one grade gets the Bell Ringer job. Last year's Bell Ringer was a sixth grader. This year, Bell Ringer is reserved for seventh-grade students.

Mrs. Taylor said, "Bell Ringer is a duty that's to be earned. It's a privilege. The student who will take on this role is the one who can best master all subjects during this school year."

At Bethune, that was me.

Mrs. Taylor told us that the decision for who would get to ring the bell is made at the end of the school year for the school year coming up. Bell Ringer is a job that starts in May, then begins again in September. Since Melanie's gone, Mr. Lloyd, the school principal, will be the Bell Ringer for now.

Mrs. Taylor called each name in her roll book,

and assigned us our jobs. Far as I could tell, the roll book names were listed alphabetically. But when Mrs. Taylor got to the *J*s, Dawnie Rae Johnson was nowhere. Finally, after somebody named Mary Anne Young, Mrs. Taylor called out my name.

Now, this is what makes no sense. Every kid sitting in that room is in seventh grade. Some of them didn't look too awake. But even the most slowpoke sleepyheaded seventh grader, even the dumbest worm in the can, knows that the letter *J* does not come after the letter *Y.* And I would bet all the dimes I've saved from my Christmas money that Mrs. Taylor knows this, too.

I was sure not going to head to the front of that classroom, snatch the roll book, and point out the right way to list names in alphabetical order.

So from now until June, Dawnie Rae Johnson will be wiping the blackboard and clapping dirty erasers every afternoon.

Friday, October 1, 1954
Diary Book.

Mama took one look at my new textbooks and said, "This is serious business, Dawnie. This school does not mess around."

I told Mama about Prettyman's baseball diamond, and clapping erasers, and how badly I want
to be Bell Ringer. She listened, but was most inter-
ested in my studies.

We laid out each of the textbooks and school
papers on our kitchen table and studied them
carefully. The papers told us what we'd be learning all year, in every subject, each month. It listed
the school principal and our teachers:

School Principal — Mr. Spencer Lloyd
Homeroom — Mrs. Vera Taylor
Math — Mrs. Barbara Hughes
English — Mrs. Jane Ruth
History — Mr. Andrew Dunphey
Science — Mrs. Polly Elmer
Gym — Mrs. Gail Remsen
And so on.

I've never seen anything like these papers.
Not ever.

The papers said things like *Algebraic Reasoning*
and *Expository Writing* and *History in Context.* There
was one word I knew for sure — *frog.* Under *Biology,*
the paper said: *Frog Dissection.*

"What's that?" I asked Mama.

"Pulling apart a frog."

"Why in the world would anybody want to pull apart a frog?"

"Biology is science, Dawnie. Seeing the parts of a frog will help you learn about innards."

The closest I've come to pulling apart a frog is *pulling* a frog from the pond down near Orem's Pasture, and *pulling* a frog back from the start line while waiting for the whistle to blow at a frog jumping contest, and *pulling* frog legs with gravy from a platter at a picnic.

I looked real good at that paper, then at the thick, shiny books with covers that cracked open and gave off a smell that said *new*.

And, oh, those book pages. Smoother than silk cleat socks.

This was why I wanted to go to Prettyman so badly. There had to be something in one or all of those silky books about how you get to be a doctor. But, Lord, did those lessons look hard, even for me.

My palms went warm. Itchy, too. It was just like before a baseball game, or when I first taught myself how to work a pogo stick.

I can *do* this. I *can* do this.

Saturday, October 2, 1954
Diary Book,

Daddy got very quiet after he finished reading today's paper. He folded it into a small, hard square, and set it on top of Mama's sewing basket for her to read. I got to the paper first, when Mama was busy with laundry.

I saw it right away — an advertisement from the owner of Sutter's Dairy, where Daddy works.

It said:

> **Sutter's Dairy**
> **Supports Segregation**
> **Join us in our pursuit**
> **for what is right in God's eyes.**

Sunday, October 3, 1954
Diary Book,

Reverend Collier gave a sermon today about the Sutter's Dairy advertisement that was in the paper.

He asked all of us at Shepherd's Way Baptist, "What *is* right in God's eyes?"

Every eye in the place was on me and my family.

Monday, October 4, 1954
Diary Book,

I have kissed my molasses lunch tin good-bye! Prettyman has a *cafeteria*. With hot food. And varnished floors. And windows big enough to show off the trees that wave hello from outside.

And buttered corn nibblets.

And mashed potatoes.

And meat loaf.

And Jell-O!

There was not a fried pickle in sight, but that didn't matter. Mama's fried pickles are the only ones worth eating.

Two ladies served the food, both Negroes. They smiled with quiet pride when I came through the line. They introduced themselves as Miss Cora and Miss Billie.

Thanks to Miss Cora and Miss Billie, my lunch plate was piled with more food than any other child's plate in that cafeteria. I got two Jell-O squares — red *and* green.

But as sweet as Jell-O and a plate full of corn nibblets can be, food doesn't taste good when you're eating all alone.

Tuesday, October 5, 1954
Diary Book,

Daddy came home from work before Goober and me even went to bed. That's usually when he's *at* work. When he pulled up to the house in his truck, he didn't come in right away. He stayed outside for a long while. "Is that *Daddy's* truck?" I asked Mama. "Why's he home?"

Mama only half answered. "He likes to let the motor run. Keeps the truck warm before turning it off."

She hurried Goober into the bathtub.

In my bedroom, she brought me a clean nightgown. "Why's Daddy home?" I asked again.

"It's time for bed, Dawnie" was all Mama said.

Wednesday, October 6, 1954
Diary Book,

It's bad enough having Bobby Hatch in my homeroom, but it's triply bad having to go to school with all three Hatch brothers. Cecil Hatch is in the sixth grade. Jeb's in fifth. Even with the grade differences between them, those boys seem to somehow travel in a pack.

They must have each been born under a full moon, 'cause goodness knows they are ugly as wolves, and just as mean.

The Hatches made today's walk through Prettyman's halls far from quiet. Those boys don't know a thing about whispering. As I was coming into the building this morning, they were ready to make some noise.

I walked in hugging tight to my books. Jeb's nose was running. He gave a hard sniff, rattled back some snot. Wiped his nose with his knuckles.

The boys let me pass with not a word from their mouths. But as soon as my back was to the three of them, they started howling after me.

"There goes Dawnie chicken lips," Cecil called.

"Got a chicken head, too, that girl," said Jeb.

Bobby said, "I'm still not sure she *is* a girl. With the way she handles a bat and runs bases, I think that chicken-lipped colored has got some boy in her."

I wanted to ram a bat at Bobby's head right then. He just wouldn't shut up. "No real girl can play baseball like that," he said.

Bobby's too dumb to know he was paying me a compliment about my ball playing. And he's too dim-witted to realize there was envy wrapped in his words. He was plain jealous of how good I am on the field.

Bobby's mouthing off encouraged the other kids standing around to start clucking. Alls I heard were their chicken noises spurting up in back of me.

Daddy says smart feet are feet that walk away from trouble. But something made me turn around right then to get a good look at those clucking kids.

For a good long minute, I watched them at the other end of that long hallway, clucking and carrying on.

Maybe it was the same something that encouraged me to turn around that also put a serious tickle on my funny bone. I had to work hard to keep from laughing! The Hatch brothers and everyone with them looked stupider than stupid, acting like chickens! And did you know that raccoons *eat* chickens? I should have brought Waddle to school!

Anyway, *they* were supposed to be making fun of *me*, but, Lord, did they look funny. I spent the rest of the day with a bust-out laugh roaring up inside me, every time I thought about Prettyman's chickens.

I couldn't let that laugh free, though. I didn't want to give the Hatches anything to get riled about. I kept my bust-out laugh trapped some-where deep in my belly.

Later

Nothing to laugh about tonight.

Daddy's lost his job.

"How come?" I asked Mama.

"Folks have threatened to boycott Mr. Sutter's business if he keeps Daddy as a worker."

I blinked.

"What's wrong with Daddy's work?"

"It's not Daddy's work that's in question. Customers don't want to support a business that employs a man whose daughter is integrating their school."

"*I* made Daddy get fired?"

"*You* make your father proud. It's the fear of ignorant people that's pushing Mr. Sutter."

"I'll go back to Bethune, then," I said.

"Stop talking nonsense, Dawnie." Mama was just short of snapping.

I shut up, but it was hard for me to not keep talking. I wanted to tell Mama I was serious about going back to Bethune. As much as I like all the pretty stuff at Prettyman, I'm messing things up for Daddy by being a student at that school.

Thursday, October 7, 1954
Diary Book,

I hate my school job! I hate it because it's stupid. I hate it because it's not fair. And I hate it because it means I miss recess, so I won't ever get to play on Prettyman's baseball field.

There are two parts to my job, which really means I have *two* jobs.

Part 1 — The Sponge:

I dip a spongy clump in the wash bucket and trail it, top-to-bottom, on the blackboard. That sponge is as big as Goober's head, and it takes a lot of two-fisted wringing to keep it from dripping all over the place.

Out the window I watch kids pushing past each other to get to the school yard. While they run, I sponge, then take the bucket down the hall to the sink in the janitor's closet, where I pour out the chalky water. That bucket is bigger than a Buick, and it bangs my leg when I walk with it. And hoisting it to the lip of the sink is no picnic.

Part 2 — Erasers:

I take them out back, near the school yard. This being my first day on the job, I started off slow. Every time the black pads slapped together, they sent out a soft thud, then a dust cloud of chalk.

Bam — pooof! Bam — pooof!

I don't do anything halfway, so I was not going to let that swelling dust get to me. But soon the *bam — pooof!* was spreading more and more *pooof* into my nose and eyes, and all around my head. A white film dusted my hair. And eyelashes. And neck. And clothes. More dusty than Mama's talcum powder.

Even though I can run a 50-yard dash without getting winded, I could hardly breathe. My coughing was louder than the hacking of a sick dog.

When I got back to class, the other kids were coming in from recess. They were shoving, and happy, and laughing from getting to be in so much fresh air.

And here's what else isn't fair. Because he's a Negro, Daddy's lost his job. Because I'm a Negro, I have to keep mine.

Friday, October 8, 1954
Diary Book,

Leave it to Mama to find a way to get chalk dust off my clothes and out of my hair. Her methods are always easy for her, but hard on me. Today she came at me with a ribbon of flypaper and pressed its sticky strip all over my clothes.

That definitely pulled up the chalk dust, but snatched at the backs of my hands near the ends of my sleeves and any other skin I had showing. For my hair, Mama made me stand by our summer house fan to let the chalk dust blow off.

And, oh, did it blow.

And, oh, did I not like it.

Saturday, October 9, 1954
Diary Book,

Mama's added something new to my Saturday chore list—raking leaves. I spend my school days beating erasers and emptying slop water, and my Saturdays doing yard work. Do kids have fun anymore?

Monday, October 11, 1954
Diary Book,

For all the staring—or clucking—kids do when I walk through the halls at school, in Math class I have the opposite problem. Mrs. Hughes, my Math teacher, ignores me.

In Mrs. Hughes's class, I'm as invisible as a ghost.

I admit, Math is my hardest subject, but I try at least. Today, each time I raised my hand, Mrs.

Hughes looked right past me. I can see that her glasses are as thick as the bottom of a pop bottle, but I know Mrs. Hughes is not blind.

During our Math lesson today, Mrs. Hughes asked us to give an example of an *integer*. Nobody raised their hand. Not one kid knew how to answer. I sort of knew how to answer, so I put my hand up, and I held it up.

The answer — I think — is that an integer is a whole number, not a fraction or a number that has a decimal. An integer can be positive, negative, or zero. The numbers 12, 3, –42, and a million are all integers. I think.

At first I thought Mrs. Hughes was giving some of the other students a chance to answer, but not one kid took the chance. I could feel the blood running from my hand. My arm started to get tired, but I was not putting it down till she called on me, or at least looked in my direction.

Mrs. Hughes repeated the question. "Can anyone give an example of an integer?"

Nobody said anything.

"Do I have any volunteers?" asked Mrs. Hughes.

Do I have any chance of getting called on? I wondered.

The room had fallen silent. No one wanted to

take a chance with the answer. They all saw my hand up. I think they were hoping Mrs. Hughes would call on me so that she wouldn't call on one of them.

Bobby Hatch burped, and everyone giggled.

We were nearing the end of the period. Mrs. Hughes went on to a new question. An easy one that even the stupidest kid could answer.

Mrs. Hughes asked, "What is a real number?"

This sent ten hands flying up. I didn't bother raising mine. It was clear I was not getting called on, even though I know that a real number is the kind of number people normally use, such as 1, 89, –37. I stayed quiet.

Here's what else I know—I have now figured out the answer to the real problem in Mrs. Hughes's Math class.

It all adds up to this:

1 white teacher + 1 Negro student + 28 white kids = 1 invisible Dawnie Rae Johnson.

Or, here's another answer to a Math class problem:

1 teacher – 1 iota of kindness = makes me feel less than zero.

P.S. This being Columbus Day, I'd have thought we'd have had the day off. But it was probably Mrs. Hughes who said, "Let's keep school open so I can make Dawnie feel smaller than a baby ant."

Tuesday, October 12, 1954
Diary Book,

In Mrs. Ruth's English class I am far from invisible. Mrs. Ruth *loves* to call on me, even when my hand is not raised. But it seems *my* understanding of English is different than Mrs. Ruth's understanding.

I mean, we're both saying the same thing—at least that's how I see it. But to Mrs. Ruth's way of thinking, every answer I give is wrong.

Today, with how Mrs. Ruth was treating me, I wondered if I was even speaking English. She asked me to name the parts of speech. Easy.

"Verb, noun, adjective, adverb, pronoun," I said. I thought for a moment. There were more, but I couldn't remember them all. "And preposition," I added.

"That's wrong, Dawnie," Mrs. Ruth said. "There are *eight* parts of speech—verb, noun, adjective, adverb, pronoun, preposition, *and* conjunction, *and* interjection."

Mrs. Ruth was right. There *are* eight parts of

speech. I'd forgotten two. But did that make my whole answer wrong?

For the next question, Mrs. Ruth singled me out again. She didn't seem to call much on other kids. Some of them even wanted to answer, but I'm the one who got all the attention. And I'm the one who got slapped down every time I spoke.

"Dawnie, what is a synonym?"

Another easy question, but I thought carefully before answering. I asked myself, *Are there eight parts to a synonym?*

I said, "A synonym is a word or a way of saying something that means the same thing as another word or another way of saying something."

That was the right answer. I just *knew* it.

"Wrong, Dawnie," said Mrs. Ruth. She looked pleased to be saying those two words together. *Wrong Dawnie.*

"A synonym is a word *or expression* that has the same meaning as another word *or expression*," Mrs. Ruth proclaimed.

Alls I could think was, *Isn't that what I just said?*

Mrs. Ruth asked, "Dawnie, are you paying attention?"

Mrs. Ruth, are YOU paying attention? This is English class, right? Are WE speaking the same language? Because

I am SAYING the exact same thing you're saying, but
saying it different, and forgetting just one small part.
But—like a synonym—we MEAN the same thing.
   Are YOU paying attention, Mrs. Ruth? Are YOU?
How about if I call you Wrong Mrs. Ruth?
   You are wrong for ridiculing me in front of everyone
when my answer is mostly right.
   I said, "Yes, ma'am, I'm paying attention."

Dear Mrs. Ruth,
   I have a gift for you—a present. (In case you
are not paying attention, gift and present are
synonyms.)
   Here are a bunch, a bundle, a heap of
synonyms for how I feel about your English class:
   Aggravated.
   Enraged.
   Furious.
   Hotter than Tabasco sauce.
   Mad as a hornet.
   Angry as a rattler.
            Sincerely,
            Truly,
            Honestly,
            (These are more synonyms, Mrs. Ru
            Dawnie Johnson

Wednesday, October 13, 1954
Diary Book,

I like my History teacher, Mr. Dunphey. He's different than the other teachers at Prettyman. For one thing, he's young and wears sweaters, not a jacket and tie like every other man teacher at school. Mr. Dunphey is definitely not from Hadley. He is no-doubt from north of here.

He greets everyone with a handshake as we enter his classroom, even me. And he addresses each of us by name, while shaking hands.

Mr. Dunphey talks funny, though. Not the same kind of funny as that lady in the black dress. He stretches my name like he's pulling a long rubber band — *Dahhhnie.*

He tells the class to pay attention so that later we can go out into the school *yaaad.* I think he means school *yard.*

I don't care what it's called, because I won't be going there any time soon.

...re that Mr. Dunphey puts a ...ny Southern name.

Thursday, October 14, 1954
Diary Book,

This evening just past supper, Mr. Sutter, from the dairy, came calling on Daddy.

Daddy stepped onto the porch. Mr. Sutter kept a distance between them. He was holding a lantern. While Daddy and Mr. Sutter spoke quietly, Mama and Goober washed dishes in the kitchen.

I went out on the porch.

Daddy said, "Go back inside, Dawnie." He was holding a lantern, too, close to his face.

I disobeyed Daddy, though he didn't know it. I went inside, but stayed near to the door screen, where I watched and listened to the two men talking.

"Evening, Curtis," Mr. Sutter said. He never once took his eyes off Daddy.

Daddy was cordial, but careful, too. "Something you need from me, Mr. Sutter?"

"How's your family?" Mr. Sutter asked.

Daddy raised his lantern. "We're getting on fine."

"You find work yet?" Mr. Sutter wanted to know.

Daddy shook his head. "I'm looking."

Mr. Sutter's lantern lit the hollows of his face.

Daddy asked his question again. "Something you need from me?"

Mr. Sutter's voice got low. "These are uncertain times, Curtis," he said quietly. "Keep an eye on your wife and young'uns."

Daddy wiped the top of his lip with the back of his hand. "Always do," he said.

Goober called me then. "Dawnie, come dry the plates."

Mr. Sutter said good night.

"Night," said Daddy.

Friday, October 15, 1954
Diary Book,

Yolanda visited today after school. She had her domino box under one arm. "Dawnie, wanna do dominoes?"

"Can't," I said. "I gotta study. I'm taking History in Context and Algebraic Reasoning and Biology now."

I showed Yolanda the paper that listed my class lessons, and I let her see my science book. "Wanna touch it? It's different from what we had at Bethune — it's *new*."

Yolanda gave me the stink eye. She looked at me like I smelled bad.

She said, "*You're* different from what we had at Bethune."

Sunday, October 17, 1954
Diary Book,

After church today, Daddy spent much of the afternoon buried in the want ads, looking for jobs. I heard him tell Mama, "All this man wants to do is support his family."

Tuesday, October 19, 1954
Diary Book,

The best part of this day was seeing Waddle, my raccoon friend, when Daddy and I walked to school. She seemed to be waiting for us when we got to Mrs. Thompson's garden. I think that raccoon's smarter than most. Her eye rings are sure beautiful.

At school, I put up with more not being called on in Math class, being picked on in English class, and being stared at everyplace else.

By the time I got home, my tree mop had never looked so good. As soon as I was done with my homework, I got my bat and *swung*! The mop did a wild dance on its rope. I batted righty, then lefty. Then righty again, twice as fast. I didn't think that mop could get any more raggedy. But I beat the strings out of that thing.

Saturday, October 23, 1954
Diary Book,

Goober disappeared today. I was helping Mama hang the wash. Goober had been hitting at the tree mop, but then he was gone. Just like that.

Mama noticed first. "Where'd your brother get to?"

She called out, but there was no answer. "*Goober*—come, child!"

I helped. "*Goob!*"

When Mama called a second time and there was no answer, she dropped her laundry basket. There was worry yanking at Mama's face. "Goober!"

Daddy hurried from inside, calling Goober through cupped hands.

"He was playing over there, by the tree," I told Daddy.

The tree mop swung slowly.

"Our front gate is still closed, so Goober can't be far off," Daddy said. But he didn't look so sure.

All three of us called after Goober. We looked for him in the cellar and underneath the porch, and behind Mama's porch rocker.

My pogo stick was where I'd last left it at the fence post, so I knew Goober had not been playing with it.

Mama's hand was pressed to her cheek. She was praying, "Lord, God . . . Lord, God . . ."

Daddy told us to all be quiet for a moment. "Stay on the porch," he said to Mama and me.

Daddy stood very still, like when he watches a cardinal or a bullfinch settle at the top of our yard's tree.

Mama sat at the edge of the porch steps. She was rocking and praying silently.

I stood by the porch post, holding on.

A ladybug could have whispered then, and we would have heard every word. That's why the rustle pushing out from the pile of leaves in the corner of our yard drew each of us to it.

And that's why I was the first to spot Goober hiding in the bundle of brown. He'd buried himself in the leaf pile!

"Goob!" I shouted. *"Oh, Goob!"*

Goober flung himself free of the leaves. "Surprise!"

There were crisp patches of brown and yellow hanging on to Goober's sweater by their stems. Dirt spots marked his elbows. He was blowing leaf pieces from his lips, and he was all full of giggles. His arms stretched high above his head. "I'm a tree!"

Mama rushed to Goober. Daddy was right behind. Me, too.

To Goober, this was all so funny.

But not to us.

Tuesday, October 26, 1954
Diary Book,

Sometimes when a special news story catches Daddy's eye, he likes to read it out loud. This morning was one of those times. He'd plunged himself into the *Hadley Register*.

He said to Mama, "Loretta, listen to this mess."

Mama filled Daddy's coffee cup before he continued. He gulped once, then he read.

First came the headline.

"'State Corporation Commission Certifies Defenders of State Sovereignty and Individual Liberties.'" Daddy took in more coffee.

He read the article next.

"'The Defenders of State Sovereignty and

Individual Liberties, a grassroots political organization dedicated to preserving strict racial segregation in Virginia's public schools, has been formed in Petersburg. Robert B. Crawford, of Farmville, has been named president of the organization.

"'Several prominent Southside Virginia leaders, including state senators Charles Moses and Garland Gray, U.S. congressmen Watkins Abbitt and William Tuck, and newspaper editor J. Barrye Wall of the *Farmville Herald*, have begun to hold meetings at a Petersburg firehouse to devise ways of fighting the threat of public school integration.'"

Mama brought Daddy more cream for his coffee. She stirred it in while he read.

"'It is the hope of these men to build a segregationist organization that will advocate for whites the way the National Association for the Advancement of Colored People (NAACP) has advocated for blacks.

"'The formation of this group comes just months after the landmark Supreme Court ruling in the *Brown v. Board of Education* case, citing segregated schools as unconstitutional.'"

Daddy set down his newspaper. He asked Mama, "What about *our* individual liberties?"

Saturday, October 30, 1954
Diary Book,

I helped Mama shell peas all morning. We sat on our porch. Our street was quiet for a Saturday. With the weather cooling, less folks stroll on weekends. Mama's raw-skinned fingers worked quickly.

Separating peas from their pods is harder than working open a shoelace knot. Peas can be stubborn. They like to hang on. I stuck with it, alongside Mama, till every pea was free. Mama hummed quietly. It was a song I knew. "Precious Lord, Take My Hand."

Sunday, October 31, 1954
Diary Book,

You can't see clouds in the dark, but you can sure feel them. I knew from the heavy smell in the air that it would rain this Halloween night. There was no moon.

Mama made Goober and me wear our raincoats. That messed up our costumes.

I was dressed as Jackie Robinson. Mama had sewn Jackie's number — 42 — onto one of Daddy's old work shirts. But you couldn't see Jackie's number underneath my raincoat. Thankfully,

Mama had embroidered "Brooklyn Dodgers" on my baseball cap.

Goober was dressed as a peanut, a costume Mama and I had built with chicken wire, brown butcher paper, and lots of flour-water paste. Mama had even made peanut shoes for Goober from old bedroom slippers she'd shined with shoe polish. Before tonight, I had never seen a peanut wearing a raincoat and slippers. Somehow Goober managed to get his slicker onto his arms. It pulled tight across the back of his costume, but had no chance of buttoning up around his front.

Yolanda was dressed as Lena Horne. In every picture I've ever seen of Lena Horne, not one of them shows her in a dress made from a bedsheet like the one Yolanda's mother had decorated with buttons, made to look like rhinestones. Each of us carried a pillowcase for collecting candy.

"You scared of haints?" Yolanda asked as we set out down Marietta Street.

"Heck, no!" I said. "I don't believe in haints, spooks, goblins, or ghosts even." The only ghoul that scares me is the Panic Monster. I didn't tell this to Yolanda.

Mama and Daddy had told us not to go past Crossland Avenue for trick-or-treating, and to make sure we went no place near Ivoryton.

When we got to the corner near Crossland, I told Yolanda it was time to turn back, time to head home. Ivoryton was right up ahead.

"I got two pennies in my treats bag," Goober said. "Two shiny pennies."

From behind us, we heard somebody making fun of Goober, repeating after him in a baby voice. *"Two shiny pennies."*

It was the Hatch brothers, Bobby, Cecil, and Jeb. They came up on all sides of us. Bobby was dressed as a cowboy. Cecil was a scarecrow. Jeb's Dracula cape stopped at his knees.

"What in the Sam Hill kind of costume is that?" Jeb was talking to Goober.

We tried to walk past the boys, but only got a few steps. They blocked us from going farther.

Bobby and Cecil bumped shoulders. They laughed. "Hey, Negro retard, what are you supposed to be?"

I prayed Goober would just not answer and keep walking, but of course he had to say something. "I'm not Sam Hill, I'm a peanut."

The brothers laughed harder. "You're a *what*?" they teased.

"A peanut," Goober said simply.

"You mean a blackie nut," said Bobby.

Yolanda surprised me then. She dropped her pillowcase, hooked arms with me and Goober, and shoved us past the Hatches.

"Run!" she hollered, holding tight. Lena Horne sure can move! Yolanda's dress flickered against the circles of light set down by the streetlamps.

Goober slowed us up. Peanuts made from butcher paper and wire can't go fast.

The boys came after us, hurling eggs.

Me and Yolanda held firm on to Goober, who was between us. "Run, Goob, run!" I encouraged.

Jeb mimicked me. "Run, *poop*, run!"

The Panic Monster was out on Halloween, dressed as himself, *shaboodle-shaking* me all over.

Eggs flew, some just missing our feet, some smacking at our backs. Thunder came. Yolanda tripped on the hem of her sheet-dress, but kept going.

When we turned onto Maycomb Street, the Hatches stopped. "That's the heart of Crow's Nest," I heard one of them say. "Pa says to never ever go there."

At the steps of our porch, Goober fell forward, hard. He was nowhere near to being hurt. His peanut's shell had protected him. His feet wiggled out the bottom of his costume. He'd lost a slipper.

Lena Horne checked the hem on her sheet.

Then it rained.

Monday, November 1, 1954
Diary Book,

I'm still shook up from what happened last night. I'm scared to tell Mama and Daddy about it. And scared *not* to tell Mama and Daddy. If I tell them, they'll ask what we were doing so close to Ivoryton, and I'll get the skin tanned off my behind. If I don't tell them, and they find out, I'll get the skin tanned off *all* of me.

This is why it's good to write things down. You can see what's in front of you and decide which way to go. I will not be telling Mama and Daddy about Halloween, or what happened last summer with the Hatch brothers at the drinking fountain.

I'll need to hide this diary good. From now on, it'll be tucked to the back of my closet shelf, behind my dictionary.

Because if Daddy or Mama reads this, I am a skinned possum!

Tuesday, November 2, 1954
Diary Book,

Last summer when Yolanda and I first set eyes on Prettyman's baseball field, I was convinced that field was heaven's front yard. I suppose heaven is a big place, 'cause today I stepped foot into heaven's parlor — the Prettyman Science lab.

The first thing I learned from Mrs. Elmer, our Science teacher, is that the word *lab* is short for *laboratory*. It sounds so official, like where you can really learn important stuff.

The Prettyman Science *laboratory* has bottles and goggles and tubes and clips and countertops — and microscopes.

And there are four sinks for washing things, and for making sure our hands are clean. Sinks in a classroom! And microscopes!

THIS is why I will put up with kids staring at me like I'm some purple-headed carnival creature, and clucking after me like they're the stupidest chickens in Lee County.

I'd bet every cent of my Christmas money that anyone who is a real doctor started out by learning science in a *laboratory*.

Today our teacher assigned lab partners. My partner is a girl named Theresa Ludlow.

When Mrs. Elmer put Theresa's name next to mine on the blackboard, Theresa was not happy. To squirm her way out of being partners with me, she told a tale taller than Paul Bunyan. Something about having a stomachache and needing to go to the school nurse's office. Mrs. Elmer dismissed Theresa, but I later saw Theresa in the cafeteria eating a hotdog covered with enough sauerkraut to stuff a bed pillow. When I get to doctor school, I hope they teach me how to cure stomachaches with sauerkraut.

I really don't care who my partner is in the Prettyman Science *laboratory*. And I don't give a toe bone about Theresa Ludlow not wanting to work with me. What I care about most is learning how those bottles and goggles and tubes and clips can teach me.

Next to the names of Science lab partners, Mrs. Elmer wrote a list of study topics we'll be learning this term — cells, germs, organs. And, just before Thanksgiving, we'll be dissecting frogs.

But first, there is lots of reading to do to prepare for what Mrs. Elmer wrote on the blackboard before the class bell rang.

FRIDAY, NOVEMBER 19 —
MIDTERM TEST

Wednesday, November 3, 1954
Diary Book,

When I got to Mr. Dunphey's History class, the desks were pushed back against the wall. *Democracy* was written on the blackboard.

"Don't sit," Mr. Dunphey instructed. "I want everyone to come to the center of the room and to stand in a circle."

Mr. Dunphey looked pleased by whatever it was we were about to do. I was curious, but fretting, too. Alls I could think was, *I hope he's not going to make us square dance.*

Well — Mr. Dunphey didn't start calling out steps for the Virginia Reel. What he made us do was worse.

He explained that we were forming a "Democracy Circle."

"Let's make this circle strong by holding hands," he said.

Kids all joined up, clasping fingers and palms. But the "Democracy Circle" ended with me. I was wedged between two students whose names I didn't know: a redheaded girl on my right, a buck-toothed boy on my left.

Not one of them would hold my hand. With the way Mama insists on me being cleaner than clean, I knew there was no dirt on my palms, but I checked to make sure. There was not even a smudge from my pencil's lead.

It didn't surprise me, or make me mad that nobody wanted to hold hands with me. Truth was, *I* really didn't want to hold hands with *them*, or anybody in this class. Just by looking, I could tell that boy's ma did not make him wash his hands. Neither did the mother of the red-headed girl.

Mr. Dunphey was eager to see the circle come together. I waited on what to do next.

Mr. Dunphey came into the circle between me and the bucktoothed boy. He took my hand in his. This still left an open space in our "Democracy Circle."

I tried to make the circle work by reaching for the hand of the redheaded girl. She flat-out refused to join hands with me.

I wiped my palm on the pleat of my skirt to get off any clamminess. Even I wouldn't have wanted to join up with a fish-hand. But the girl wasn't having it. She balled up her fingers and held her fist tight at her side.

Mr. Dunphey, he's clever. He put a classroom chair between me and the girl, and told us to each hold on to the back of the chair. The girl looked relieved.

Mr. Dunphey said, "By forming this circle, we represent the people of America, joined together under our nation's guiding political principle — democracy.

"This circle represents what democracy stands for — that we are all equal. None of us is higher or lower than the other. Democracy is the standard that makes America's government unique. The chair I have set between Dawnie and Jennifer represents the seat of government, the place where a government exercises its authority. It's where key political decisions are made. America's seat of government is Washington, D.C., our nation's capital."

I was glad to have my hand on the seat of government, but there was no kind of *democracy* at Prettyman that I could see.

When Mr. Dunphey gave my hand a gentle squeeze, I felt something I have not ever once felt for a teacher. I felt sad for Mr. Dunphey. He really believed what he was trying to teach us about democracy.

But when you go into a store and can't try on the clothes, when water fountains won't let you drink from them, and when you're the only Negro student in a school where every day you eat lunch alone, democracy is as far off as the moon.

Later

Tonight I looked up *democracy* in my dictionary.

Here's what I found:

Democracy: A fair and equitable government by the people.

Dear Mr. Webster:

I have a question about your definition of democracy.

Which people do you mean?

Thursday, November 4, 1954
Diary Book.

Heaven's parlor has lost its shine.

Today in the Science laboratory, we got to use our microscopes to look at cells.

To see the cells, we had to put blue liquid onto a glass slide, then place the slide under the microscope's viewer.

Theresa and I had to share a microscope. Even though I was super-eager to see the cells, I let

Theresa go first. I don't think she even cared about looking at the cells. She put her eye to the viewer, blinked, and said, "Your turn."

I pressed my eye to the microscope's viewer. Those cells were beautiful clumps of jewels, swirling together in the pocket of blue liquid that brought them into view.

I watched the cells dance and play together. But the party ended when I felt something warm and wet, then burning, pouring onto my lap.

It was the blue liquid we'd used to put on our microscope's slide—all over the front of my skirt! Snatching at my thighs, making them itch, heating my skin.

I sucked in a hard breath. Cut my eyes at Theresa.

I raised my hand. Mrs. Elmer must have seen me wincing. She came right over. She looked at me sharply, then at Theresa.

"It was an accident," Theresa said.

Accident, my eye!

Tripping on a tree root coming up through the dirt is an accident.

Going to the wrong address 'cause you wrote the number three instead of the number two, that's an accident.

Theresa Ludlow pouring blue cell juice onto the front of my skirt is no accident.

It's what Daddy calls *intentional* — Theresa meant to do it.

Mrs. Elmer brought a cold compress. She gave it to me to wipe the burning blue from my thighs. "Don't worry, it's not dangerous," she said.

The cold cloth soothed my legs right away, but *I* was still burning.

I spent the rest of today going from class to class with a blue splotch down my front, putting up with kids' snickers.

When I came home from school, Mama gasped. I told her all about the "accident."

Mama tried every way possible to get that stain out of my skirt, but even she couldn't get rid of the blue.

"Wool holds on," she explained. With disappointment and disgust both tugging at Mama's expression, she told me to throw the skirt away. "Even if I could get it clean, I do not want that memory in my house."

Dear Theresa Ludlow,
  You meant to spill that Science lab liquid on me. You intended *to do it. I know that. That*

blue juice made me red-hot-orange mad!!

Theresa, more than anything, I want to pour a jug of that blue stuff all over your head. I want to watch you twist in your seat 'cause your skin itches and your clothes are messed up. I want your mother to have to throw away one of the few skirts you own. I want this badly.

But, Theresa, I will not pour anything on you. I will not, 'cause I have a better plan. My plan is called DAWNIE RAE JOHNSON'S INTENTION.

Pay attention, Theresa, 'cause this is no accident.

I intend to do well in Science.

I intend to be a good student at Prettyman so that I can become a doctor.

I will not let you stop me from reaching my dream. I INTEND this.

This letter should really be a thank-you note.

To you, Theresa Ludlow.

Thanks to you, DAWNIE RAE JOHNSON'S INTENTION is stronger than ever!

Friday, November 5, 1954
Diary Book,

I thought I would die from chalk dust today. I have made a decision — another *intention*. I will do whatever studying it takes to earn my way to that Bell Ringer job.

Later

More flypaper from head-to-toe, getting the chalk off my clothes. Hair blowing in the wind of our house fan. How does Mama think of these things?

Saturday, November 6, 1954
Diary Book,

It's warm for November. I have just come in from being outside, at the tree mop, where I beat that stringy thing silly with my baseball bat. Half past ten, that's the time. Lights-out is long gone. Everyone's asleep.

The moon is a softball, pitched high up into the curtain of black sky that hangs over our house. If my bat could reach, I'd swing and knock that ball free until it fell and tumbled to the place in our yard where the tree mop swings from its raggedy rope.

For now, I'll let that softball moon spread its white light, right here into my bedroom, giving me the light I need to fill your pages with my determination.

Monday, November 8, 1954
Diary Book,

I miss Bethune. I don't miss the broken toilets and the stopped clocks. But I miss learning in a place where teachers talk to you, and smile, and say "honey" and "darlin'" when they speak your name. And I miss just *being* at school, not *being a Negro* at school.

I miss teachers who call on you in class and work hard to help you get the right answers. And who know you're paying attention and trying your best.

Those are the same teachers who can always find a way out of no way. Even with ripped books, they taught us somehow. I miss the simple dignity everyone has at Bethune, and the self-respect we were made to have by our teachers.

Here's what else I miss — every man, woman, and child at Bethune has beautiful dark skin, same as mine. They are all shades on the colored rainbow — everything from butterscotch to baker's chocolate, all sweet. Nobody looks at you funny at Bethune.

And — every man, woman, and child who steps foot in that school takes pride in knowing about Mary McLeod Bethune and what she accomplished and stood for. I miss that, too.

If you ask any kid at Prettyman who their school is named after, they'll tell you that Ronald Prettyman was a rich Virginian who made his money in the pork rind business and built the school so he could have a building named after himself.

As bad as I want to learn what it takes to be a doctor, and as keen as I am to someday get myself into college, I am doing it by attending a school built from the skin of pigs.

Wednesday, November 10, 1954
Diary Book,

Daddy's still out of work. Mama's taken in extra laundry. Our house is filled with sheets and table linens and collars and cuffs. After school, I help Mama hang shirts to dry.

"Two clothespins at each shoulder," she told me today, pressing the pins onto the bleached cotton corners, showing me how it's done. "There's more wind at this time of year," Mama said.

Our wash line has become a parade of sleeves, waving at the Virginia breeze, flapping hello in the cold.

Friday, November 12, 1954
Diary Book,

Today when I emptied the chalk water in the janitor's closet sink, I set eyes on the best sight ever. It was a small thing, but a big thing, too. I don't know where it came from, but there it was, tucked into the crevice where the sink meets the wall — a Jackie Robinson baseball card, same as mine!

Oh, and now I know why the hall floors of Prettyman shine so brightly. Our janitor, whoever he is, has got five mops, standing proud as a parade, in his closet.

Saturday, November 13, 1954
Diary Book,

The only time I've ever heard Mama and Daddy argue was when Daddy told Mama that from now on he was only putting a penny in the collection plate at church because he had a feeling that some of his hard-earned money was going into the gas tank of Reverend Collier's Pontiac.

Tonight, after the dishes had been cleared and washed, Daddy and Mama had angry words between them.

Goober and I had long since gone to bed, but I hadn't been able to sleep.

Too much on my mind.

Daddy said, "White folks have been against us for too long, Loretta. When I was a boy, they humiliated my own daddy, and he felt powerless. My father couldn't keep whites from undermining him. And nothing's changed. Now *I* feel powerless. I can't get a job because of the hatred of those people and their feelings about Dawnie integrating Prettyman. With her at that school, how am I supposed to earn a living and keep my integrity as a man?"

Mama was quick to speak. "Curtis, this isn't *about* you!"

Daddy tried to get in the next word, but Mama wasn't having it.

"Loretta—"

"*I'm* talking now!"

Daddy got quiet.

Mama said, "What do you mean, nothing's changed? *Everything's* changed, and Dawnie's making that change possible. Our daughter wants this. She's as smart and as capable as any of those white children, and she deserves what that school has to offer. Have you seen the books she's bringing home? The materials are better at Prettyman. That school's got higher-level math. And a Science lab."

That made Daddy even madder. "Somebody needs to go into that Science lab and whip up a peace potion that will make all kinds of people get along."

Mama said, "Where's your faith, Curtis? I'm taking in extra laundry. We'll make ends meet. Work at Sutter's Dairy, or any job, doesn't give you your *integrity as a man.* Dawnie is being watched over with the might of angels, and so are we. I believe that. The Lord has chosen our child to be at that school."

Daddy snapped, "I know it's not Dawnie's fault, but where were those angels when I lost my job?"

Now Mama was really yelling. "Enough, Curtis! *Enough!*"

Goober must have heard Mama and Daddy fighting. He came into my room. Folded himself into the corner near my night table.

Without looking, he reached up, fished around the night table's top. He slid my pink curlers onto each one of his fingers.

"They hurt," he said.

Monday, November 15, 1954
Diary Book,

Today Daddy walked me to school, like always.

Waddle was waiting. She watched and listened to me and Daddy talk.

I blurted, "It's because of me that you got fired, isn't it? I'm going back to Bethune."

I started to cry, but yanked in a hard breath. Bit hard, too, on my lip.

You would have thought a baseball had smashed through the front window of a car. Daddy stopped walking. Just like that. He knelt down to where he could look me in my face.

"It's *because of you* that I have the strength to keep my head up," Daddy said. "It's *because of you* that I told Mr. Sutter he could let me go, that I was not pulling my daughter out of a school where she belongs, and has a right to attend." Daddy thumbed my chin. "It's *because of you* that I walk the path to Prettyman every morning with the pride of ten men."

"But —"

Daddy put a finger to my lips to shush me.

"*But* is a word best left to doubters, quitters, and weak-willed souls. *I* am not a doubter, Dawnie. *You* are not a quitter. *We* are not weak willed."

162

Daddy stood up. He cupped my hand, gave it a gentle tug. And we walked.

Tuesday, November 16, 1954
Diary Book,

Daddy's right. I'm no doubter or quitter. But today I was tested on both those things.

When I got to Science class, Mrs. Elmer told us to take our seats quickly and that she'd be handing out our midterm tests. "Get settled, students, we don't want to waste any time getting started," she said.

"The test is *today*?" I asked.

Mrs. Elmer set my test sheet in front of me. "Today" was all she said.

There was no time to flip through my assignments log, but I was as sure as I am that my name is Dawnie Rae Johnson, that the mid-term Science test was scheduled for Friday, November 19, three days from now. That date had been written on the blackboard. That date had been entered into my assignment log by me. That date had been dancing around my dreams for weeks.

I tried to protest, but having a teacher think you're being disagreeable is never a good idea. I didn't want to sass Mrs. Elmer. I just wanted to make sure I was not the one making the mistake.

"But—you said—you wrote—" was all I could manage.

"I *said* the test is today, Dawnie."

Other kids were beginning to write their test answers.

Mrs. Elmer came over to me. I did my best to whisper. "Back when we started class, you wrote on the blackboard: 'FRIDAY, NOVEMBER 19— MIDTERM TEST.' That's what I recorded in my assignment ledger."

"Are you back-talking me, Dawnie?"

"No, ma'am."

Mrs. Elmer explained, "The test date change was announced last week before everyone lined up for recess."

"That's when I clap erasers," I told Mrs. Elmer. I wasn't whispering anymore. "I never heard about the change." I'm no crybaby, but my voice had a whine to it.

Mrs. Elmer said, "It's your responsibility to stay up on assignments, Dawnie. Besides, your lab partner was supposed to apprise you of the new test date."

The time for taking the test was sliding away quickly. I was already behind. I needed to get started, or I wouldn't finish the test.

I set my pencil to work, but was it ever hard to concentrate! This was worse than being shoved into a cold pond when you're not expecting it, and landing face-first with a smack.

I was writing my answers fast and furious. I couldn't *think* about the answers, though. I'd studied for the test, but getting ready for a test takes more than just knowing the facts. I need the warm-up in my mind — spending a minute picturing myself taking the test and doing good on it. And holding that picture in my thoughts till it's all I see in front of me.

I didn't *have* a minute, though. By the time I'd begun, I had less than twenty minutes to take a half-hour test.

The only warm-up in my mind was the thud of a headache starting as I tried to see the test questions clearly.

Then something changed.

Somewhere between filling in the blanks about the nervous system and respiration, the thud in my head turned to punching in my chest. At first, I thought it was my heart pounding past my ribs. But it was more than that — it was my *intention*. Then came the same voice I'd heard when Mama and I first set eyes on the papers that explained what my science lessons would be.

You can *do* this? You *can* do this?

The voice grew louder. My intention, simpler. *You can.*

I raced through my answers, filling in the last question one second before Mrs. Elmer announced our time was up. The punching, pounding intention in me said, *You did.*

Wednesday, November 17, 1954
Diary Book,

When Mr. Dunphey, my History teacher, sees me in the hallway, he says hello. At dismissal, Mr. Dunphey says good-bye to all the students. He doesn't leave me out, like some of the other teachers do. Mr. Dunphey is a person with manners.

Today in class, Mr. Dunphey called on me. He asked me to describe the three branches of government. I was startled by the question. Not because I didn't know the answer, but because he asked the question so frankly. I could tell by the kindness in Mr. Dunphey's way of talking that he wouldn't twist my answer, like Mrs. Ruth does in her English class.

I said my answer to Mr. Dunphey's question

clearly. "Legislative, judicial, executive."

Mr. Dunphey nodded. "Good," he said. "Now, stand up, *Dahhhnie*, and repeat your answer so that we can all hear it," he encouraged.

I did what Mr. Dunphey said, plain and simple. This teacher made me feel like a regular student. It was almost as good as sliding into home base.

Friday, November 19, 1954
Diary Book,

Every Friday I ask myself how I made it through another week at Prettyman. Mrs. Elmer gave back our graded test today. I got every answer right, but didn't get a 100% on the test.

Mrs. Elmer handed back everyone's test but mine. With one test paper left from her pile, she asked me, "Is this yours?"

In glancing quickly at the page, I could see that every question was marked as correct with a check mark. I looked closer, and soon saw why my paper said "98%" on top. Mrs. Elmer had spelled it out in red:

MISSING NAME

MISSING DATE

I'd been so rushed, I'd forgotten to fill in my paper's very top line. That cost me two points.

I admit — it's not good to forget your name. But as far as the date goes, I sure as heck do not want to remember the day of that surprise test!

Saturday, November 20, 1954
Diary Book,

If leaves were pennies, I'd be on my way to the rich man's bank. I raked more leaves today than I knew could even live on a tree. I saved two of the prettiest ones, a yellow leaf with red veins, and a red leaf with a yellow stem. They're opposites, but the same. While Mama pressed sheets and shirts for her customers, she let me iron each leaf into a square of waxed paper. I looped a string of yarn through the top of each leaf and hung them in my bedroom window. When the light hits them just right, those leaves are as bright as the stained-glass windows at Shepherd's Way Baptist Church on a sunny day.

As much as I hate raking, there is one more good thing that came out of today's leaf pile. I found a frog.

I've never seen a frog smile, but this frog looked glad when I scooped him up, then set him down in the shoe box where my Vaselines once lived.

I felt it was only fair to warn the frog that he

wouldn't be in the shoe box for long, and that he would be devoting his life to a higher purpose.

I've never seen a frog cry, either, but I would have bet all the pennies I'd put in that rich man's bank that this little rust-colored critter was shedding some froggy tears when I told him the news.

Tuesday, November 23, 1954
Diary Book,

If I ever do become a doctor for people, I will tell my veterinarian friends to treat frogs kindly. Frogs have sure paid their dues for the sake of science. Today we dissected frogs as part of our Biology lesson. Nowhere on the school paper about what lessons we'd be learning did it say that the school would be *giving* us frogs to pull apart. I'd brought my frog from the leaf pile to school, and kept him in his shoe box all morning.

When we arrived in the Science laboratory, each of us had a frog at our place—an already-dead frog. The ugliest frogs ever! My own frog must have smelled his dead cousins. He'd been quiet and still all morning, but was now bumping the sides of the shoe box.

When Mrs. Elmer asked about the shoe box,

I explained that I'd brought a frog from home for the Science lesson on frog dissection. The other kids tittered, and even I thought it was funny. Mrs. Elmer put my shoe box on her desk during our lesson. She shook her head, looking not-too-pleased.

The already-dead frogs were the palest pink, and scrawny. By the looks of them, they'd been fed some bad flies, and had died of amphibian indigestion.

Those frogs had had a hard life, it seemed. They could not have been from the pond near Orem's Pasture, or Hadley even. And, those already-dead frogs were the stinkiest things. *Hoo-boy. Stink-eee.*

Each frog was on its back, arms spread, eyes open, mouth wide. And, man sakes, the frogs had already been sliced open, down the belly! The way those frogs' eyes were rolled upward, I was certain each one of them had been praying to heaven before being killed in the name of Biology.

Mrs. Elmer instructed us to first wash our hands, then to put on the safety goggles. Then she walked us through our lesson. She kept calling the frogs "specimens."

We had to look at a large frog line drawing at the front of the room, and identify our frogs' stomachs, livers, and hearts. I think my frog from the leaf pile was watching out one of the holes I'd cut into the sides of his shoe box. He was tap-tapping during the entire class. Nobody seemed to notice but me.

As sorry as I felt for those already-dead frogs, I liked poking around their innards. My frog's stomach swelled out from him like a little balloon. Now I know where all those flies go. And by looking real close at the belly of my already-dead frog, I could see how fried pickles work their way through my own tummy. I like this thing called "biology."

After class, Mrs. Elmer gave me back my shoe box, which I kept under my desk until the school day ended. As soon as I got home, I let my frog free into the pile of leaves. There is no doubt he was wearing a frog grin.

"Get on, now," I warned. "Prettyman's on the lookout for specimens!"

Later

At supper, I told my family about the already-dead frog, and the frog's pinky innards. I even drew a picture on my napkin, just like the picture in our classroom.

Mama said, "No drawing at the table."

Daddy said, "Let the child show off how much she knows."

Goober asked, "Do frogs eat peanuts?"

Wednesday, November 24, 1954
Diary Book,

At school, I broke Daddy's rule about keeping my hands to myself.

I couldn't help it. That Jackie Robinson baseball card in the janitor's closet has been looking at me every day for weeks. And every day, I've been asking myself, *Why would somebody just leave a Jackie Robinson baseball card out like that*? Seems the card *wanted* me to touch it. As soon as my hand was on the card's corner, peeling it out from its crevice, I found out why it had been put there.

Today I met Mr. Williams, our school janitor. "Jackie keeps me going" was his way of introducing himself when he came into the closet and caught me holding his card. We shook hands. I told him my name.

Aside from the lunchroom ladies, Miss Cora and Miss Billie, Mr. Williams is the only other Negro I've seen at Prettyman. "You make the fourth to ever set foot in this building," Mr. Williams said.

And he told me something else, too. "Dawnie, you and Jackie Robinson have a lot in common."

Thursday, November 25, 1954
Diary Book,

Thanksgiving break. I'm grateful for our tree mop, fried pickles, and my pogo stick. Today, when I bowed my head for Daddy's Thanksgiving prayer, I whispered a quiet gratitude, "Lord, I am most thankful for four days of freedom from chalk dust and murky eraser water!"

Friday, November 26, 1954
Diary Book,

Mama wastes no time bringing on Christmas. Our tree goes up the day after Thanksgiving. Tonight we decorated that tree from its pointy top to the lowest branches. Goober ate half the popcorn meant for stringing. But we still had plenty of balls and bows to cover every limb.

This year Mama made decorations to represent each of us. For Goober, she created a wreath made of peanut shells. For me, a strand of felt-cut bells that we looped along our banister. Daddy's decorations were shredded newspaper strips pulled into pom-poms.

"Where's *your* decoration?" I asked Mama. "What did you make to show who you are?"

"Come see." Mama led us to the porch, where she'd built a miniature Christmas village, constructed with clothespins. There were even clothespin reindeer and a clothespin sleigh.

We spent the rest of the evening eating Thanksgiving leftovers. Tonight when Mama came to my room to kiss me before bed, she held me for a time, and sang, *"Dawnie, Dawnie, sweet potato pie."*

Saturday, November 27, 1954
Diary Book,

Reverend Collier called a special meeting this evening at church. Shepherd's Way was filled with lots of people I didn't know. They'd come from congregations throughout Lee County, and were eager to fill our pews. There were Negroes, white folks, boys and girls, and babies bundled tight. I spotted people from Calvary Baptist, the church whose team we whipped last summer in baseball at Orem's Pasture. That boy Lonnie gave me a quick wave.

Daddy explained that the white folks were all from the NAACP. I recognized the lady and the men who'd come to our house.

Somebody needs to tell the NAACP lady to stop wearing mud-colored lipstick. At least her dress wasn't black. Tonight she was wearing a suit the same color as peas. There were other white ladies, too, all dressed like her. And men with big-collared suits.

Mama made me wear the Peach Melba dress and the Vaselines. Since she'd worked so hard on giving me Christmas bell decorations, I didn't make a stink about the dress and shoes. At least the dress fits now, and I didn't have to do much walking in the Vaselines.

Reverend Collier asked our family to sit in the first-row pew. We were one pew up from the NAACP people. The NAACP lady put a gentle hand on Mama's shoulder when we got to our seats. A man I didn't know shook hands with Daddy.

Reverend Collier said, "This will be a night to remember at Shepherd's Way. We have a very special guest here this evening."

People clapped. The man who'd shaken Daddy's hand rose and made his way to the pulpit. He stood next to Reverend Collier, who introduced him. "I am very pleased to welcome a young preacher from the Dexter Avenue Baptist

Church in Montgomery, Alabama. He has just been named the pastor at Dexter, and has come to address us this evening. Please welcome young Brother Martin Luther King, Jr."

The applause grew. I'd heard of Martin Luther King. He was just starting out as a preacher. Folks had been talking about him. He had a powerful way of speaking.

Martin encouraged us to become active members of the NAACP, and to vote in government elections. He spoke about the importance of peace and his belief in something he called "nonviolence." There was brass and thunder in his delivery. I could not take my eyes off this man. His strong-strong way of speaking scooped me up and held on.

"Praises be!" somebody shouted.

Another voice rang out. "Amen, Brother Martin."

But people also expressed doubts about Martin's ideas of nonviolence. Yolanda's father said, "With all due respect, I'm not one for standing by and letting white people hurt us."

"Praises be to *that*!" came a voice from the back of the church. It was Mr. Albert, who sells peanuts from his cart.

Martin told us that love and unity will move

Negro people forward. And that fighting for justice and equality can be done quietly, without weapons, or hatred.

"Tell it, young brother!" someone called out. "Tell it!"

Others protested loudly, and soon our church became a swarm of debate, with people taking sides. Goober covered his ears from all the yelling. Martin raised a hand to quiet the noise.

Reverend Collier spoke next. That's when I saw why we were sitting in the first row. He pointed at Daddy. "This is a man whose livelihood has been threatened because he has taken a stand against segregation by allowing his daughter to attend this town's white school."

More applause rose up. Martin Luther King clapped, too.

Reverend Collier said, "Brothers and sisters, I return to a question I asked in this church months ago—who among us steps back in the face of a threat?"

The reverend talked more about threats. And he spoke about Daddy. And about me.

"Mr. Sutter, who owns Sutter's Dairy, is a man who has *stepped back*. His customers had threatened to boycott, to take their business elsewhere because Brother Curtis and his daughter, Dawnie, and the Johnson family, have been brave enough to *step forward* toward progress."

Applause, louder this time.

"When Mr. Sutter let Curtis go, his white customers stayed loyal. But what Mr. Sutter must have forgot is that Negroes buy as much butter as whites, and that a good chunk of his business comes from *our* side of Hadley and Negroes living in nearby towns, and throughout Lee County."

Reverend Collier's delivery now came on as strong and as booming as a drum. He was truly sermonizing. "We know what it means to boycott, too! We have what it takes to pull our business away from Sutter's — to *step forward* peacefully, but powerfully."

Goober had not taken his hands away from his ears. And it was a good thing, too. There was all kinds of yelling going on.

"How's boycotting Sutter's gonna do anything?" Miss Nora, Roger's ma, wanted to know. "Why should I have to give up cream for my tea, on account of that too-good-for-the-rest-of-us child sittin' up at Prettyman, not staying with her own for schoolin'?"

I'm good at lots of things, but I'm not a *too-good-for-the-rest-of-us* child!

"*She* started this mess." Miss Nora was pointing at me. "Let *her* miss out on some milk."

Somebody else shouted, "We need to take a bold step! Boycotting butter ain't bold!"

With the help of Martin, Reverend Collier quieted everyone.

Our reverend tried to reason with the doubters. "Boycotting is nonviolent, but it'll hurt Sutter — in a quiet way. We'll be putting a hard pinch on his wallet. After a while he'll feel the pain."

Some of the NAACP people and Reverend Collier gave us very simple but perfectly direct instructions.

"Starting Monday, when the milkman comes, refuse to take his bottles. If he leaves them on your porch, don't use the milk. Let it spoil."

People listened.

"Don't purchase any butter, cream, or cheese," the reverend instructed.

I was all for nonviolence and for helping Daddy, but no milk, butter, cheese, or cream?

That sure *was* a pinch — just thinking about it hurt as much as sleeping in curlers. Martin led us in a prayer. Miss Eloise, our choir director, stood.

She played on a tambourine, and started to sing "I'm on My Way."

The congregation joined her. The song swelled, rising through the church with the tambourine's rattle.

When I glanced at Daddy, he looked like he'd just won a prize at the fair. He was so pleased. Mama, too. And Goober — he'd found a church fan and was waving it and singing. He had the tune right, but had changed the words to *"No more cheese for me!"*

I sang, too, but I was not ready to say good-bye to buttered toast and mac-and-cheese.

Monday, November 29, 1954
Diary Book,

First day back to school after turkey and pie. I dragged my feet to the breakfast table.

Dry toast didn't help. Daddy drank his coffee black. Goober filled his oatmeal bowl with cider.

When Daddy and I walked to school, Waddle was waiting in her usual spot. Dawn's blue curtain made it hard to see her fully. But the streetlamp's light showed off the double rings that formed Waddle's raccoon mask.

Waddle's fur's gotten thicker, her tail bushier.

She looks thick, too. Big around the middle, storing fat to keep warm for the cold months ahead. Winter's not far off. "Nice coat," I said to my raccoon friend.

Even by afternoon, I had to wear mittens for clapping the erasers. I smacked them together with a fury to get it over with quickly. White *pooof* rose all around me, from the chalk dust, and from the steam that spewed warm into the icy air as I coughed.

Saturday, December 4, 1954
Diary Book.

It snowed lightly during the night. Powdered sugar on our grass. Goober had his coat and mittens on already when he brought me my pogo stick. "Teach me, Dawnie." He shoved the stick at me. "*Show* me. There's no more dirt. The stick won't get stuck. It's all white now."

"It'll be slippery," I said.

But Goober was right. The ground was hard enough to make the pogo go. With winter coming, I knew this would be one of the last times I'd be jumping on my pogo stick, so I gave Goober another lesson, with the snowy ground beneath us.

First I showed Goober how to jump on, then off the stick, two feet at a time.

"Watch me. On — off." I demonstrated for Goober, who hardly let me finish, he was so eager.

Goober copied me. "On — off!" He did good on the first try.

We worked our way up to five full bounces. Goober was able to jump a little bit forward. "Am I flying, Dawnie?"

"You're flying good, Goob."

"On — two, three, four — off!" Goober was all smiles, even though the spring on my rickety pogo stick was squeaking the whole time.

A few tries at pogo-flying were enough for Goober. When his nose started to run, he was ready to go inside.

I've set my pogo stick in my bedroom closet, where it'll sleep till spring.

Sunday, December 5, 1954
Diary Book.

I woke up this morning to the promise of winter.

We don't get lots of snow in Virginia, but when snow covers all the houses and trees, and spreads a quilt thick enough for making snow angels, I'm the first one to sing about jingle bells.

Yolanda came over after church today, bringing gingerbread baked by her ma. We made up a song about the snow, and sang it together:

Fluffy silver stuff, stuff, stuff
Makes a ball of puff, puff, puff
Will it be e-nuff, nuff, nuff?

Yolanda and I giggled and giggled. She saw for real that I am not uppity.

Monday, December 6, 1954
Diary Book,

The milkman came today, early, before the sun, like always.

He left the six glass bottles of milk in our tin collection box on the porch.

Oh, did I want some milk with my oatmeal!

At cafeteria time, I was tempted to drink from the Sutter's milk carton that comes on our lunch trays. Miss Billie delivered me from temptation by not putting the milk on my tray. She also left off the pudding, and gave me a burger without cheese. If I didn't think the kids at Prettyman would ridicule me, I'd have brought my lunch in the Peach Melba pail with the bow on top.

Later

Ever since the boycott started, our phone has been ringing more than before. When Mama answers, no one speaks. Tonight eight calls came, with silence on the other end of the line.

Tuesday, December 7, 1954
Diary Book,

Here is my Christmas list.

It's called *Dawnie Wants*.

1. *Dawnie Wants* a new pogo stick.
2. *Dawnie Wants* Daddy to get a new job.
3. *Dawnie Wants* a glass of milk and some mac-and-cheese.
4. *Dawnie Wants* to be Bell Ringer.

And here is the rest of the *Dawnie Wants* list, for my eyes only.

5. *Dawnie Wants* to kick Bobby Hatch in the teeth.
6. *Dawnie Wants* Mrs. Elmer to slip on a wet floor and break her collarbone.
7. *Dawnie Wants* Theresa Ludlow to wake up with warts.

Thursday, December 9, 1954
Diary Book,

Back came the milkman to take the bottles from Monday, and to deliver new milk. It was so cold outside that the milk probably didn't spoil. Still, the man in the Sutter's truck set out six bottles of fresh temptation. Is it ever hard to not drink that milk!

Friday, December 10, 1954
Diary Book,

The telephone has been ringing all evening. Only three of those calls have been from people we know. The rest were hang-ups. We only have one phone. It's on the wall next to our refrigerator. With all the ringing, our phone seems to jangle the whole house.

I can tell by the way Mama's snapping for us to keep out of her kitchen, and to fold the laundry faster, and to do our homework, and to get ready for church on Sunday, that she's agitated.

Goober's getting on Mama's nerves. I just know it. He's annoying me, too. Walking in fast circles, pretending to answer a telephone, repeating, "Hello . . . hello . . . hello . . ."

Finally, this evening, Mama took the phone off

the hook so that we could eat supper in peace. But Goober wouldn't let up.

"Hello . . . hello . . . hello . . ."

Except for saying grace, we ate with hardly any words between us.

Goober kept on.

"Hello . . . hello . . . hello . . ."

Finally, I couldn't take anymore. I yelled at Goober almost near to cursing. "Goober, shut the heck up!"

Saturday, December 11, 1954
Diary Book.

Mama and I went to the post office in town today to mail Christmas packages to my aunt Karen, Mama's sister in Tennessee. We ran into Miss Nora, Roger's loud mother. Mama was cordial.

"Happy holidays, Nora," she said.

Miss Nora was not feeling the joy of the season. "It's hard to be happy when you can't use cream to make eggnog," she huffed.

"Try canned milk," Mama suggested.

"Try sending Dawnie back to Bethune," Miss Nora huffed.

Mama was working hard to stay nice. "Nora,

it's too late for that now. Besides, nobody's *making* you boycott Sutter's."

Miss Nora held tight to her parcels. "My boy Roger has twisted my arm. I'm just glad we've kept him at Bethune. You're courtin' trouble, Loretta," Miss Nora said. "I would not want to be standing in your shoes now."

"Believe what you believe," said Mama. "I believe my shoes are walking in the right direction."

I couldn't help but turn my eyes to what Miss Nora was wearing on her feet. She had her nerve! Those were the ugliest shoes ever. They looked like warty toads, with shoelaces.

I would not want to be walking in *them*.

Sunday, December 12, 1954
Diary Book,

Who put Miss Nora on hospitality duty at our church's front door?

Seems she invited one of her friends to join her in putting me down.

Miss Laura, a lady from our church sewing circle, stood next to Miss Nora as we filed into the entry at Shepherd's Way.

This must be the season of ugly feet.

Miss Laura's shoes were as black as my Vaselines, but no kind of shiny. She must have picked them up from the giveaway pile on the Wicked Witch's front curb.

Mama nodded to both women. "Ladies, good morning."

Miss Laura's greeting was as sharp as her shoes. "Well—hello to the too-good-for-the-rest-of-us Johnsons."

Not that again.

Reverend Collier started services by asking everyone who was participating in the Sutter's boycott to raise their hands.

Some hands went up right away. Many stayed down. But after a moment, all hands were raised. All of them! Roger had both hands raised.

That made me want to raise both *my* hands.

So I did.

Monday, December 13, 1954
Diary Book,

Today we were sent home with two flyers from school. One announcing something called the "Bell Bake Sale," the other reminding students about final tests for the semester. The Bell Bake Sale is to raise money for a new bell that will be stationed outside the school building on the front lawn. The flyer showed a drawing of the bell. That is a *big* bell. It's housed in a brick well, and swings from an iron hinge. The handle for ringing the bell is as big as the grip on a butter churn. Just by looking, I can tell that bell rings loud enough to slice the clouds.

I reminded Mama about my miserable eraser job and about the Bell Ringer job I really want. As soon as she read the flyers, she put on her apron. "I'll start baking, you start studying," she said.

Soon our kitchen table was covered with sugar, bowls, textbooks, tablets, flash cards, and flour.

I asked, "How we gonna make sugar cookies with no butter or milk?"

"Canned milk and Crisco oil," Mama said.

Canned Crisco Sugar Cookies. That sounded yuckier than yucky. If one person bought one of my cookies, I'd be lucky.

"But, Mama—"

"But nothing, Dawnie. Let's get started."

Mama wasted no time. She mixed the ingredients, kneaded cookie dough. I memorized state capitals.

Then we switched. I got busy with the rhythm

of our rolling pin. Mama worked with me on algorithms.

We baked enough cookies to feed all of Hadley. We let the Math facts flow. We sprinkled and studied. And tasted and tested. The Canned Crisco Sugar Cookies were sweet and good.

As I write this, I'm exhausted, but ready for the Bell Bake Sale and any bonus test questions thrown my way on semester finals. And — I'm ready for that bell. That big, beautiful bell.

Tuesday, December 14, 1954
Diary Book,

One of the great things about a bake sale is that nobody knows who's baked what. My Canned Crisco Sugar Cookies stood among all the baked goods for the Bell Bake Sale. I didn't tell a soul that those glittery cookies came from Mama's kitchen. If I haven't learned anything else at Prettyman, I've learned that the kids at that school will do whatever they can to undercut me.

I watched with silent satisfaction as those cookies sold. Since Mama and I had made so many — and since they were the tastiest cookies ever — they earned the most money for our school. It made giving up milk and butter worth it.

My end-of-the-term tests went well, too. I whipped through state capitals from Boise to Nashville. Fractions — easy. Word problems — no problem.

Mr. Lloyd, our principal, announced the successful sale of so many sugar cookies, and told the whole school the bell was on order and would arrive by spring.

I came home with an empty cookie tray and a mind filled with knowing my stuff.

Wednesday, December 15, 1954

Counting
A Poem by Dawnie
Counting days till Christmas.
Counting days till spring.
Counting days till Dawnie Rae gets a new bell to ring.

Thursday, December 16, 1954
Diary Book,

Today's erasers spewed enough chalk dust to coat my tongue. Thank goodness Mama'd kept some of our cookies at home for all of us to enjoy.

I licked the red-and-green sugar crystals off two cookies. It was their sweetness that let me taste how unfair the bake sale was. My cookies had earned the most money to help *buy* the school's new bell, but I can't *ring* the bell.

P.S. I haven't seen Waddle for some time now. Daddy told me that raccoons don't truly hibernate in winter, but they do sleep more, and only come out a little bit in cold weather. I wish I were a raccoon.

Friday, December 17, 1954
Oh, Diary Book!

I'm writing so fast. And shaking. And my head hurts. I can hardly believe today.

Goober came to Prettyman to meet me after school. He'd come on his own. Another one of his surprises! I was leaving out the back way, which cuts to the street quicker. I spotted Goober far off at the place where Prettyman's playing field ends and the railroad tracks begin.

I could hardly believe what I was seeing. Goober was waving with both arms. He had my pogo stick in one of his hands, waving that, too. He jumped onto the pogo's pedals, pumping, then falling off, then trying again. From where he was, I could hear the squeak of the pogo stick's rickety spring.

He called out to me, "Look, Dawnie! Look at

me! I can pogo, even when there's a whole mess of snow!"

I raced to him. "Goober, what are you doing here? You're not supposed to come out past our fence without first asking Mama or Daddy or me, not ever! And you're not wearing a hat or mittens."

I was super-angry at Goober, but I worked hard not to show it. He cries when I yell at him. The last thing I needed was for Goober to cry.

I yanked him off school property as fast as I could.

I have to wonder — are we wearing some kind of magnet that pulls the Hatch brothers to us? We were two blocks past Weedle Lane, and there they were! Again. The three of them — Bobby, Cecil, and Jeb!

I can't even write all what they said. I don't want to remember it, so I won't put it on paper. But I will tell you this — only because if I don't, I will break open from holding on to today as an ugly memory.

The Hatch brothers threw Goober down in the snow. Bobby punched Goober twice. Once in the stomach, then once in the nose, until it started bleeding. Then all three boys ran off.

The wet on my face from crying was stinging my skin, and making a frosty film from the wintry air. I sniffed once, hard. I didn't want Goober to see me really crying.

I helped Goober up. He was yelping from the pain, and rubbing at his nose. I pressed my scarf to the place where his bloody nose still dripped.

Mama was right about Goober. He sees the world in his own way. I tried to encourage Goober to put his head back to stop the bleeding. But he was too fascinated with the snow.

"Look, Dawnie, look. Do you see it?"

"See what, Goob?" I said softly.

"It's pretty, Dawnie. It's red, like a flower. Like a rose with white all around it. It's so bright in all the white-white."

"Yes, Goob, I see it." I couldn't keep from crying, no matter how hard I tried.

Later

Mama gently rubbed salve on the inside of Goober's nose, and on the outside place where Bobby Hatch had punched him.

Goober let out a tiny moan. He flinched, then was silent.

Daddy held me while we watched Mama dab witch hazel.

That night I did some punching of my own. It started with my baseball mitt.

I rammed my mitt onto my left hand, then punched into its fold, hard, with my right.

Bam! Bam! BAM!

Something slammed at me right then, 'cause the punching grew to an all-out attack with my fist. I couldn't stop.

BAM! BAM! BAM!

My punching hand got redder and redder and started to hurt me bad. But the *BAM! BAM! BAM!* kept coming.

Both my hands were shaking with a rage. Soon all of me shook. I roped both my arms tight around myself. A throb pulsed into both my fists, till I fell asleep on top of my bedcovers.

Saturday, December 18, 1954
Diary Book,

Goober's gone somewhere I can't reach. He's locked himself off in a place that's deep inside him, and has slipped down a silent hole. He won't talk. This morning I unfolded our checkerboard, set it up with peanuts as playing pieces.

"Goob, wanna play?"

Goober rocked in his seat at the kitchen table, eyes looking past me to where only he could see.

"Leave him be," Mama said.

Sunday, December 19, 1954
Diary Book,

After what happened to Goober, Mama and Daddy have put my pogo far back in our cellar's canning closet. They said it's too dangerous to leave it in my bedroom closet, where Goober can find it.

"You're not to play with that stick, or even go near it," Daddy said sternly. "Do you hear me, Dawnie?"

I understood why Daddy was being so strict, but winter passes quicker when I can at least *see* my pogo stick.

Mama said, "You can take it back out in May for your birthday. You are not to look for it before then." She was firm. "That stick stays where it is until the eighteenth of May."

"Yes, Mama," I said.

May is forever from now. The *eighteenth* of May is more than forever away.

The only thing I can do is wait.

Monday, December 20, 1954
Diary Book,

I tried to make Goober laugh tonight before bed, but it was no use. I put my curlers on each of my bare toes, and danced the Slop. He didn't even crack a smile. He watched me dance, though, with a quick flick of his eye following my sloppy toes.

Wednesday, December 22, 1954
Diary Book,

Goober's nose is badly bruised.

So are my knuckles from punching.

Friday, December 24, 1954 – Christmas Eve

Dear Santa,
Here is a new Dawnie Wants *list:*
1. Dawnie Wants *Goober back.*

Saturday, December 25, 1954 – Christmas

Dear Santa,
Thank you! I got my Christmas wish.

Goober padded into our living room with woolen feet. He yanked his Christmas stocking off the banister. It was filled with peanuts. He cupped a bundle in both his hands, offered me a bunch.

"Happy Christmas, Dawnie!"

My Christmas stocking jangled with fifty pennies, ten nickels, and five dimes—a whole $1.50! I've put the coins inside my Vaselines. That's the only good use for those shoes.

Tuesday, December 28, 1954
Diary Book,

My report card came in the mail today! I made the honor roll. I have pasted my report card here!!!

PRETTYMAN COBURN SCHOOL
Mid-Year Academic Report

Student: Dawn R. Johnson
Grade: 7

Markings This Term:

Math: B
English: A–
Science: A
History: A

So yeah, they can trick me into taking a test on the wrong day. They can ignore me in Math and keep me hopping in English.

I may not be a super-duper genius, but I know what I know. What I know is that when I bat, I'm playing to win. Same for school.

Prettyman, pitch as hard as you want, 'cause I'm going for a home run.

Wednesday, December 29, 1954
Diary Book,

My name is in the *Hadley Register* for making the honor roll. And what'dya know — they've listed the students alphabetically, and I'm in the right place with the *J*s. I sure hope Mrs. Taylor reads the paper.

Our phone is back to ringing. All day.

Today I answered it.

There was a voice coming through the receiver.

A muffled man's voice.

"Milk bath," he said.

I hung up quickly.

"Don't answer that phone!" Mama scolded.

Friday, December 31, 1954
Diary Book,

Here it is, the last day of the year, and the front page of the *Hadley Register* carried this headline:

Hadley School Superintendent Takes Action to End Integration

Says the Negro Influence is Tarnishing the Learning Effort

The article said integration has come too fast to Hadley, that segregation is the natural order of things, and the "rapidity with which integration has happened has caused social and emotional unrest for the students at Prettyman, thus making it difficult for them to learn."

I looked up *rapidity* and *tarnish* in my dictionary.

Rapidity: The quality of moving, acting, or occurring with great speed.

Tarnish: To make dirty. To stain. To soil.

The only thing occurring with great speed is how fast I've been able to get good grades at Prettyman. If this has "tarnished the learning effort" of those other kids, then they weren't too smart to begin with.

Rapidity, stupidity.

Past Midnight

We went to midnight church services to celebrate the coming of a new year. Reverend Collier made an example of me in front of everyone. From his pulpit he congratulated me for making the honor roll. He then referred to the newspaper article in the *Hadley Register* about the school superintendent wanting to end integration.

Boy, did the reverend preach tonight! He gave a sermon that started in the final half hour of 1954 and lasted through the first hour of 1955! He referred to the article again and again. He called me up to stand next to him in front of everybody. "And here," he proclaimed, "is the Negro influence!"

I really don't mind church, but our family seems to be getting a lot of attention. No wonder Yolanda's gone sour on me. After services, Yolanda came up close behind to where I was standing. She spoke so only I could hear what she had to say. She poked me at the waist. "This here," Yolanda whispered, "is the uppity influence."

Yolanda Graves has turned sometime-y. She's become one of those friends who's nice sometimes, and sometimes not nice. The problem with sometime-y people is that you never know which sometime they're on—nice or not nice.

Saturday, January 1, 1955
Diary Book,

I'm glad I made the honor roll, but this New Year doesn't feel happy, or new. We're pushing the same old rock up the same old hill. At night I dream about Goober's blood piercing the snow.

And about the Hatch brothers turning into haints.

And about Daddy working at Sutter's Dairy, and getting eaten alive by a giant cow.

And Yolanda calling me uppity sometimes, and sometimes singing and making snow angels.

I'm bone-tired from not sleeping good. I'm hot-mad-angry, too.

This is not a New Year to celebrate.

If Jack and Jill went to the top of Hadley's same old hill, not even fetching a pail of water could put out the slow fire burning in me.

Sunday, January 2, 1955
Diary Book,

It's the in-between, and I'm restless. I'm so glad to have this Diary Book. The book and my red pencil have become good friends. I need friends now.

The sky is purple, same color as a scab. That means more snow. I don't like more snow. More snow gives me nightmares about Goober's bloody nose staining the white.

My window has set that scab-colored sky behind a screen of gray, put there by the radiator's steam. The radiator paints the glass with its hot breath.

Back to school tomorrow.

Monday, January 3, 1955
Diary Book,

There's a new girl in my homeroom class. Her name is Gertie Feldman. Gertie Feldman is not like any white girl I have ever met. She *tawlks* like that lady from the NAACP. She speaks to grown-ups like she knows them. There's nothing shy about Gertie Feldman.

At lunchtime today, Gertie was behind me in the cafeteria food service line. When Miss Cora and Miss Billie served my plate with the most food of anybody, then served Gertie with the same measly portions every other student gets, Gertie wasted no time telling them she wanted what I had. "And more gravy, too," she insisted.

Miss Cora and Miss Billie exchanged a sharp look that could only mean they have never witnessed a child like Gertie Feldman.

When Gertie came to sit next to me, she said, "You get this whole table to yourself?"

Before I could explain that the lunch table has been my own since September, Gertie was *tawlking* about how much she liked the gravy.

The other kids in the lunchroom had their eyes all over Gertie and me. She didn't seem to notice or care. The best part about so much *tawlking* from Gertie is that she was quick to tell me she's moved to Hadley from Brooklyn, New York, the home of Jackie Robinson's team, the Dodgers! She was proud of it, too.

And — Gertie's father is a doctor!

When her mouth was too full of potatoes to speak, I was able to ask two questions. Gertie's answer was the same for both.

"Have you ever seen Jackie Robinson play?"

Gertie slurped her chocolate milk.

"Lots."

I let her swallow before asking, "Have you ever seen a colored doctor?"

The last bit of chocolate milk gurgled through Gertie's straw before she said, "Lots."

Tuesday, January 4, 1955
Diary Book,

The only place I've seen more grease is at the bottom of Mama's skillet after frying bacon, when Mama collected that thick yellow gunk to unstick my pogo spring.

This morning Mama was on a Vaseline mission. She would have shined my snow boots if I hadn't begged her to put that jumbo jar of goop away. She was determined to slather my face, though. "Keeps the cold from chafing," she said. "Protects you from wind."

Mama had my cheeks squeezed tight in the grip of her folded hand. And, oh, did she smear. Even with my squirming, Mama was putting a shine on me that glistened more than a basted turkey. "Hold still, Dawnie!"

I had no choice but to stand there and take it. She even spread the Vaseline on Daddy, who let her do it without complaining one bit.

When Daddy and I left for school, it was cold.

"That stuff works, doesn't it?" Daddy said as we faced the windy street, still cloaked in darkness.

My hood was tied tight under my chin. January's bluster met us straight-on.

Okay, I admit—Brother Wind was no match for my basted-turkey face.

Waddle was waiting for me today. She's lucky to have a face full of fur. No grease for her.

Later

I'm awake, writing fast.

Tonight after supper the phone rang six times. Mama didn't answer it. Daddy, either. I know *I'm* not supposed to answer the phone, but this whole thing is riling me. On the seventh ring, I grabbed for it. Daddy tried to coax the receiver from my hand, but it was too late.

A man's voice whispered the same strange message as before, "Milk bath."

I hung up quickly. Didn't tell Daddy and Mama what I'd just heard.

I'm guessing this all has to do with the dairy boycott.

Tonight I'll be sleeping with the light on.

I'm scared to death!

Wednesday, January 5, 1955
Diary Book,

Mrs. Taylor must have gotten a note from Santa telling her that she needed to be more nice and less naughty. Today Mrs. Taylor told me that I could clean the erasers during Study Hall, so that I could go to PE in the gym with my class, which replaces the recess period I was missing last term.

The only thing is, I still have to find time to study somehow. Maybe I can clap the erasers fast, then make it to Study Hall for half the period. I'm sure not gonna worry my mind over it. With winter here, and me having no recess all last semester, I was feeling like a cooped chicken at school. But starting tomorrow I'm going to PE. Finally!

Thursday, January 6, 1955
Diary Book,

Mama says that high expectations lead to low serenity. That was sure true today. PE at Prettyman is for babies! This afternoon we did something called "calisthenics" — jumping jacks, toe touches, and arm circles. What kind of mess is that? We ended the period by hauling large blue mats onto the gym's center floor and participating in what

Mrs. Remsen, our PE teacher, called "tumbling." Each one of us had to take a turn doing somersaults down the length of the mat.

I'm no Charles Atlas, but I can do a bunch more than arm circles, toe touches, jumping jacks, and somersaults.

You wouldn't know it, though, by watching me today. Thanks to Mama's Vaseline, my somersaults were the slipperiest bunch of tumbling ever. Each time I pressed my head to the mat, my greasy scalp sent me sliding!

This did not sit pretty with the other Prettyman girls. When they saw my oil patches left on the mat, they wanted to quit the tumbling. Mrs. Remsen wouldn't let them, though. She made them somersault, one after the other, behind me. The only one who didn't make a stink about it was Gertie, who out-tumbled us all.

Saturday, January 8, 1955
Diary Book,

I guess every white family in Ivoryton wants clean clothes to start the year. Mama's been under a mountain of laundry. With the weather being so cold, we hang the wet clothes on racks in our cellar. But we're low on racks and space to hang. Our living room has turned into a haunted house of sheet ghosts and headless dresses, hanging from ceiling rafters, dancing above our radiator's steam.

"What if they boycott *us*?" I asked Mama.

"Then the Lord will provide some other way," Mama answered, sounding sure.

Daddy said, "Your Mama's laundry service is the only one — and the *best* one — within miles. Some white people can be mean, but they know what's good when it comes to laundry."

Monday, January 10, 1955
Diary Book,

I AM NO MONKEY! I AM NO ELEPHANT! I AM NO DOG!

If going to PE means I will have to put up with stupid girls, then I'll stick with eraser clapping. At least when I clap erasers, there's Mr. Williams, who treats me kindly.

Today in the girls' locker room, after I had changed into my gym suit, I had to pee before going out into the gym. Mama had warned me quietly that whites don't like us using their bathrooms, and that I should always be mindful of this when I feel the need to relieve myself. Most school days I hold it from morning to afternoon, then gush as soon as I get home. But today I couldn't keep it in. So I went.

I knew something was strange when the locker room grew silent when I squatted to urinate. As soon as I let loose, I heard muffled giggles and whispering coming from someplace above my head. I didn't want to look up. But how could I not?

Looking over the top of the stall was Theresa Ludlow from Science class, and four other girls. I yanked up my panties and gym bloomers, but it was too late. They'd seen my bare bottom already. Theresa said, "I thought monkeys had tails. Where's your tail, Dawnie?"

Another girl, Jennifer Little, the redheaded child from Mr. Dunphey's "Democracy Circle," answered, "Maybe Dawnie's *not* a monkey. I mean, she's such a big-boned girl, I would think she's got an elephant's tail."

They all laughed. Then two more girls whose names I didn't know started making barking noises.

"Didn't you know?" one girl asked the others, "All Negroes have dog tails. Maybe Dawnie's tucked hers away in her underpants."

Mrs. Remsen's whistle sounded right then, and

the girls scurried away to the gym. I waited till I heard the door to the gym rattle closed. When I came out from the stall, I kicked hard at the lockers. I wanted my baseball mitt. I wanted to punch.

I sat for a moment on the locker room bench, punching at my knees. I could hear the girls' squeals and shouts echoing in the gym. I made my way to join the rest of the class.

Gertie was waiting for me. "You look like you've seen a ghost."

"No ghosts in there," I said. "But plenty of witches."

Mrs. Remsen's whistle blew for the second time. Now she was blowing it at me. "Dawnie, you're late. Take twenty laps around the gym."

I didn't flinch. Mrs. Remsen had done me a favor. I started off slow, then sprinted, while those baby witches tumbled their somersaults.

Wednesday, January 12, 1955
Diary Book,

Daddy has taken to helping Mama wash, fold, and iron. He complains that this is "women's work."

I love my daddy, but that is a backward idea. God gave hands to men and women. Except for bigger palms and longer fingers, a man's hands can do the same things a woman's hands can do.

The same is true the other way around—except for softer skin and nicer cuticles, a woman's hands are the same as a man's. Ironing and folding clothes can be done by anybody *with* hands.

I hope Daddy gets a job soon.

Friday, January 14, 1955
Diary Book,

Gertie called out to me as I was walking home from school.

"Dawnie, wait up." Her coat was made from the thickest wool plaid I've ever seen. It was a nice coat. She fished a black licorice twig from her pocket. "Want some candy?"

I am never supposed to take candy from somebody I don't know well, and I'm sure not supposed to eat candy on a regular day that's not a holiday. But Gertie wasn't really a stranger. And, one licorice twig was more like a snack, not a treat.

Gertie chomped and talked and walked alongside me.

"Where you going?" she asked.

Where else would I be going?

"Home," I said.

"Me, too," said Gertie.

Gertie was with me for most of the whole two miles as we made our way closer to Crossland Avenue.

When we got to the place where Ivoryton ends and my neighborhood begins, Gertie kept walking. Now I was the one asking, "Where *you* goin'?"

"Home." Gertie handed me another licorice twig. Red this time.

"Where's your house at?" I wanted to know.

"Maple Street," Gertie said.

I stopped walking. So did Gertie. "What's the matter?" Gertie asked.

"You live in the colored part of town?"

Gertie shrugged. She looked puzzled. "I guess I do."

Man sakes, I was witnessing a strange miracle — a white girl who does not live in Ivoryton.

I explained all about Ivoryton and Crow's Nest, and how the neighborhoods work in Hadley.

"That's just stupid," Gertie said.

At the corner of Crossland Avenue, me and Gertie waved good-bye. "See you tomorrow," she said. She handed me a third licorice twig. Another black one. It was sure sweet.

The ball on top of Gertie's hat bobbled as she walked away.

Monday, January 17, 1955
Diary Book,

A letter to the editor appeared in today's *Hadley Register*. Here it is:

Dear Editor,

Thank you for your coverage of the recent events surrounding integration. I have lived in Hadley all my life. This is a peaceful town. We have enjoyed the goodness of neighbors and friends. As a mother, I have always done right by our three children, and have made their well-being my top priority. This includes their education. But now, with this push for integration, school has become a bad place for my children. It will only get worse if we let integration continue. There is good reason to keep schools segregated. Colored children learn differently than white children. Coloreds are slower, and less capable of grasping certain concepts. It is unfair to white and colored children to mix them together, especially in a school setting. By doing so, we rob each of them the opportunity to learn as best they can, and we ruin any chance we may have for keeping our town one of this state's finest.

Signed,
Anonymous

I read the letter twice, then I looked up *anonymous.*

Anonymous: Having an unknown name or identity.

Tuesday, January 18, 1955
Diary Book,

I don't agree with the letter from that unknown mother with the three kids. But she's right about one thing. Integration has robbed people and ruined chances.

Because I'm attending Prettyman, nobody will hire Daddy in Hadley. Not even black people. Everyone's afraid that employing Daddy will somehow bring them trouble. Today he drove as far as Richmond looking for work. He came home with his hands in his pockets, his head down, and no job. Tonight I heard him tell Mama that somehow, some way, word has traveled that his child is the one integrating the schools in Hadley.

When Daddy goes asking for work, he should tell the people his name is Mr. Anonymous.

Wednesday, January 19, 1955
Late Night
Diary Book,

Somebody threw a glass milk bottle at our front door. It smashed onto our porch, splattering milk everywhere.

I will be sleeping with the light on again.

Thursday, January 20, 1955
Diary Book,

The phone won't stop.

My prayers stay strong.

I'M SCAREDER THAN SCARED.

Friday, January 21, 1955
Diary Book,

Another letter to the editor of the *Hadley Register* appeared today. It said:

Dear *Hadley Register*:
We are living in the modern age. We have television. And we even have frozen TV dinners. Scientists have found a way to launch a rocket ship.

These are all great advances in scientific progress, but they don't account for human progress. We slow human progress by trying to go against natural forces. If race-mixing were meant to be, then blacks and whites would be able to get along much easier. This has never been the case. Coloreds make it hard to like them, or to trust them. They are mean and dishonest people.

"Whites Only" signs serve an important purpose. These signs should be posted at Prettyman Coburn. Integrating our schools allows for the influx of boys and girls who come from a disreputable clan of people.

Sincerely,
Lester Rudd, President,
Hadley Business
Owners' Association

I have never met Lester Rudd, but I think he's very confused. I have never seen a frozen TV dinner. Why would anyone want to eat a dinner that's frozen and shaped like a TV?

Sunday, January 23, 1955
Diary Book,

The phone woke us this morning. Four rings in a row. Then silence. Then four rings more. We all came into the kitchen. None of us answered the phone. Daddy was in his bathrobe still. With his tool kit, he carefully dismantled the phone. He took the whole thing off the wall!

Now the phone never rings. Daddy's hushed it for good.

Wednesday, January 26, 1955
Diary Book,

Another day of Vaseline cheeks and slippery somersaults. Today Gertie asked me how I get my skin so smooth. "Vaseline by the ton," I said.

Thursday, January 27, 1955
Diary Book,

Gertie and I walked home again today. She had a pocketful of gumdrops, all colors. But our walk turned from sweet to sour as soon as we got off school grounds.

Somehow the Hatch brothers had hooked up with Theresa Ludlow and her friends—the PE class witches—and they were following us from behind.

Theresa started off with the troublemaking. "A colored *and* a Jew, both at our school. That's a bad combination," she said.

Next came Jeb Hatch, calling out, "I think I smell fish."

Cecil said, "That's not fish, that's how dirty Jews smell."

I started to walk faster, but Gertie was slowing down. Then she just stopped, dead in her tracks.

She turned to face those boys and the witches, and stepped right into the center of them. I have never seen a white girl stare down a white boy with such fury. Gertie got right up in Cecil's face. "*What* did you say?"

All my insides were clanking. The Panic Monster had his *shaboodle-shake* on full blast.

Nobody said anything.

Gertie just kept glaring. One of the witches said, "Better not mess with her. She may put some kind of Hebrew hex on you."

Gertie leaned in. Cecil backed away. So did his brothers and the other kids. So did my Panic Monster.

Gertie turned toward home, walked past all of them, her shoulder bumping through the wall made by the group.

"C'mon, Dawnie, let's go home," she said.

Right then, on what was probably the coldest day in Virginia, I was warm as coals stoking a pot-bellied stove.

Later

I asked Mama, "What's a dirty Jew? And what's a Hebrew hex?"

Mama looked horrified. "Where in the world did you hear such disgusting talk?"

I knew anything coming out the mouth of a Hatch boy, or one of those witchy girls, had to be bad. But I wanted to ask the question just how they said the words, so I'd get the full, real answer.

Mama said, "If I *ever* hear you talk like that again, I will wash your tongue with lye, do you hear me, Dawnie?"

I told Mama all about Gertie Feldman, and the Hatch brothers and Theresa and her friends. "Gertie lives on Maple Street, down by Orem's," I said.

Mama sat me down. She explained the history and culture of Jewish people, and the persecution they've endured. She told me about a man named Adolf Hitler, and World War II, and something called the "Holocaust." "It is an ugly story," Mama said.

Now *I* looked horrified. I knew nothing about Jewish people. I thought white people were white people, and if they had different religions, it didn't matter because they were white.

I had no idea that whites hated other whites because of their religious beliefs. Living in Hadley, all I knew was that most white people hated Negroes, and the same was true the other way around — most Negroes did not like whites.

Well, I now had a white friend. And she liked me, too. So, as far as Gertie and me were concerned, there was no other way around it.

With all due respect to Mama and Daddy, I don't believe there is no hate in God's eyes. Has God seen the Hatch brothers and Theresa Ludlow, and their friends? They are full of HATE! HATE! HATE!

They probably invented the *H* word! And I HATE it!

Friday, January 28, 1955
Diary Book,

Gertie came to school with more shine than me. "I tried the Vaseline," she said. "How does my face look?"

Gertie had caked the stuff too thick. Even her eyelashes were gloppy.

In the girls' room, I helped her thin down the Vaseline by spreading my palm across her forehead.

Now Gertie Feldman is a city slicker who's not *too* slick.

Monday, January 31, 1955

Dear Mr. Jackie Robinson,

    Happy Birthday! If my figuring is correct, today you're thirty-six. That's as old as Daddy. Did the Dodgers help you celebrate? If I was invited to your birthday party, and you let me blow out the candles, I'd wish for a job for my daddy.

                Filled with wishes,
                Dawnie Rae

Tuesday, February 1, 1955
Diary Book,

The other thing I really miss about Bethune is Negro History Week. Yolanda told me that starting Monday, seventh graders at her school get to pick their favorite "Notable Negro" and give an oral report in front of the class.

If I was still a student at Bethune, I wouldn't have to think twice about the subject for my oral report. I wouldn't need to study or practice, either. I can speak good about what colored people have accomplished. I would be happy to give a speech.

The Panic Monster takes a vacation during Negro History Week.

There is no Negro History Week at Prettyman Coburn School. There is no Negro History anything at Prettyman Coburn.

Wednesday, February 2, 1955
Diary Book,

Very early. Before the in-between. My throat hurts.

Missing school and having to make up work will hurt worse.

Prettyman, here I come.

Thursday, February 3, 1955
Diary Book,

Feels like I've swallowed a rusty saw. Oh, my throat!

I spent much of today wishing I could put my head down on my desk and sleep. I'm sure my classmates would've laughed from here to Halifax County at the sight of me drooling onto my books. Thankfully, there was no drool, only a long day at school.

Friday, February 4, 1955
Diary Book,

That rusty saw has met up with a heap of cotton inside my head. My ears are more stuffed than Mama's pin cushion. I'm so tired. I've been moving slow all day. Thinking slow, too. What was Mrs. Elmer saying about bacteria? I bet that'll be on Monday's Biology test.

Saturday, February 5, 1955
Diary Book,

Spent the day coughing, sniffling.

Monday, February 7, 1955
Diary Book,

This morning I woke up with a nose so red, I could have been mistaken for a circus clown. I must have sneezed ten times before rolling over on my pillow. My sheets were clammy, too. When I looked out my bedroom window, there was a whole mess of hurly-burly snow flying sideways. I could tell by the rattling of my windowsills that there was some mean wind outside. Still, I was hot as heck when I sat up in bed.

Morning was full-on bright. "What time is it?" I asked Mama.

"You're staying home from school today," Mama said, bringing me tea and two handkerchiefs.

It is every child's wish to hear her mama say she's staying home from school. And I'd be lyin' if I didn't admit there have been times I have prayed for the croup so I could miss at least one day of school. But couldn't the day be next week — *after* my Biology test?

"I'll stay home tomorrow," I told Mama, kicking off my sheets.

Mama's hands came on fast, sliding my bedcovers back near to my chin. "You've got a cold, Dawnie, and you shouldn't be spreading it."

I told Mama about the test, and how missing the test would hurt my grade.

"I'll send a note to the school, explaining," Mama said. She tried to comfort me by adding more honey to my tea, but a bathtub of honey could not have sweetened the ache I felt from having to miss my Biology test.

Then Mama brought a jar of camphor rub and started gooping it on my chest, under my nose, and behind my ears. I thought Vaseline was bad. But camphor — *yeech!* That stuff is sure powerful! Its fumes could clear the pipes on the crustiest church organ in Lee County.

I never, ever thought I'd write this — but more than anything, right now I want to be sitting in Mrs. Elmer's class answering questions about how bacteria grows!!

February - ?
Diary Book,

Home from school again. Swallowed the rusty saw all day. Cotton on the brain. What day is it? Too weak to write more.

Saturday, February 12, 1955
Diary Book,

Two more milk bottles were thrown at our house tonight. Two more quarts of hate. Skidding onto the snowy floor of our front porch.

Daddy's taken to spending nights propped in a chair by our front window.

Watching through our curtains.

Trying to keep us safe.

Saturday, February 19, 1955
Diary Book,

Goober's made me a red paper heart that's as big as his head. When I told Goober Valentine's Day has come and gone, he said, "Love is all the time, Dawnie."

Sunday, February 20, 1955
Diary Book,

More sideways snow.

The tree mop's strings are a frozen clump of cold, stuck to an icy rope.

How many days till May?

Monday, February 21, 1955
Diary Book,

Feeling better. I *begged* Mama to let me go to school today. If she'd have allowed me to get out of bed for something other than to use the bathroom, I would have gone to Mama on my knees, saying, *please, please, please.*

"You'll go back to school tomorrow," she said. "One more day at home will do you good."

This must be what jail feels like. I hate being stuck at home.

At least the snow has melted. As I write this, the sky outside is a beautiful shock of bright blue. My waxed-paper leaves are showing off their colors, their opposite-but-same yellow and red veins.

Mama loaned me a wax pencil from her pattern-making kit. I have decided to name my leaves. I wrote their names at the top of each.

Dawnie's the one in yellow. Gertie's wearing red.

Tuesday, February 22, 1955
Diary Book,

People say if you can smell something bad on yourself, it really stinks. I knew I'd be showing up at school today smelling like camphor. Mama would only let *me* go back to school if I agreed to let her make me the Queen of Camphor.

Whew, is that stuff powerful! The only things smellier were the already-dead frogs from Biology class.

No wonder the snow has melted. The camphor fumes must have seeped from our windows onto the streets. Today its odor rose so high off my clothes that even the neighborhood dogs ran in the opposite direction when they smelled me coming.

Same with the kids at school. More than usual, they did their best to avoid me.

Gertie was glad to see me, though. "Camphor" was the first thing she said when I slid into my homeroom seat next to her. "My papa uses camphor rub on me when I'm sick," Gertie said.

"Your daddy the doctor uses camphor?"

Gertie nodded. "Rubs it all over me, like he's waxing a car."

I will not be telling Mama that a real true doctor uses camphor. If she ever finds out, she will for sure keep me steeped in that stuff.

Gertie had volunteered to clap erasers and sponge the blackboard when I was gone. She said, "There's only one good thing about that bad job — Mr. Williams, the janitor."

Today I was back to clapping the erasers on my own. When I got to Mr. Williams's closet to dump my chalk water, he helped me lift the bucket to the lip of his sink. "Missed you," he said.

He smelled me right away. He said, "Camphor's good for the soul."

Later – After supper

Daddy showed me a *Look* magazine article about Jackie Robinson. In the picture, Jackie's holding his bat high over his shoulder. I clipped that photo and pasted it to my bedroom mirror. I can see why they put Jackie in *Look*. He sure *looks* strong.

Daddy's grown restless trying to find a job. While I did my homework, Daddy went outside in the cold dark nighttime. He took my bat with him. From where I sat at our kitchen table, I could see Daddy out our back window, swinging and swinging at my tree mop.

When I finished my homework, I asked Mama if I could go outside with Daddy, expecting she'd say no. But she let me. I yanked my hood strings tight at my neck, put on my mittens.

Daddy and I took turns batting righty.

Wednesday, February 23, 1955
Diary Book,

Today in Mr. Dunphey's History class, we talked about current events. Bobby Hatch brought in the *Look* magazine article about Jackie Robinson. He stood up, waving the page with Jackie's photo. "I don't care how many runs Jackie Robinson's had," Bobby said. "He should've stayed playing with coons. That's why there's a *Negro* League. The game is called baseball, not *blackball*."

The other kids laughed.

"Bobby, stick to the article, please," Mr. Dunphey said. "What's *current* about what you've read?" he asked.

Bobby did something I have never seen a kid do. He smart-talked a teacher, right in front of everybody. Bobby said, "What's *current* is that the major leagues *currently* have a new song to sing. It's called 'Darkie in the Dugout.'"

Something ripped through me then. Something so powerful it could have only been what Mama has called "the might of angels."

My chair screeched when I stood up at my seat. I was glad my throat was better. I needed to speak. Negro History Week is over, but colored people make history every day, so I had a lot to say.

I talked, talked, talked about Jackie Robinson and the accomplishments of notable Negroes. I kept talking. And Mr. Dunphey let me. I told everybody about Mary McLeod Bethune and Thurgood Marshall, one of the lawyers from the New York paper. During my time at Prettyman, I'd held on to my gift of gab for too long. Today was the time to use it.

Everybody got quiet. Bobby looked like he'd swallowed a baseball. He could have thrown a dozen eggs at me right then. I would have caught each and every one of them, and hard-boiled all twelve with the heat rising up in me.

But not one egg flew in my direction. Not even

a word came from the other students. Everybody was too busy listening.

Whether those other kids would admit it or not, I had given them their first Negro History lesson. Gertie was smiling big.

When I was finished, I said, "That's all Dawnie Rae has to say."

Thursday, February 24, 1955

Dear Mr. Jackie Robinson,

I told my History class about you. Since then, something's changed in that class. The air seems different in Mr. Dunphey's room. Better somehow. Maybe I'm different. And better.

Yours,
Dawnie

Saturday, February 26, 1955
Diary Book,

Boy, the editor of the *Hadley Register* must have a very full mailbox.

Tonight Daddy pointed out another letter in the paper. This letter is not anonymous, or filled with wrong ideas. This letter is brave. And smart. And true. I have pasted it here.

To the Editor:

I became a History teacher because I believe that the past provides a vital key to the future. The founding fathers of our nation spent long days in the Philadelphia heat of summer authoring a document that would serve as the definitive statement on all that America stands for. This document became the Declaration of Independence, a roadmap, if you will, for how we are to conduct ourselves within the auspices of all that America holds dear. The Declaration of Independence also makes it clear that under the laws of nature and of nature's God, all men are created equal, that they are endowed by their Creator with certain unalienable rights, that among these are life, liberty, and the pursuit of happiness.

By denying Negro children entry into any school they wish to attend, we slap the faces of our founding fathers. We trash their intentions. We soil what it means to be American.

When I moved to Virginia from Boston last summer and was offered the chance to teach at Prettyman Coburn School, I came expecting Southern charm. I looked forward to small-town life and to the courtesies afforded those who call the South their home. It was my hope, too, that I could someday share my passion for American history with young people of all races, sitting side by side in the same classroom.

Segregation is an evil and corroding thread. If we allow segregation to continue, if we give power to its iniquity, we risk the immoral.

If we are to live comfortably within our own skins, we must push past the prejudices of skin color. If we're to create a future for ourselves and our children that promises life, liberty, and happiness, then we must turn our backs on segregation. We must, as it says in the concluding sentences of the Declaration of Independence, "pledge our sacred honor" to embrace the promise that integration offers.

Among those who made this pledge on July 4, 1776, and who signed their names to America's most prevailing document, seven were Virginians, including Thomas Jefferson.

Let us now follow their example. Let us now turn our backs on the scourge of racial hatred. We, the residents of Hadley, have a tremendous opportunity. That is, to show America that the state of Virginia is a great beacon of democracy.

Very truly yours,
Andrew Dunphey,
History teacher,
Prettyman Coburn
School

It's late. I should be asleep. But this letter has made me squirrely. My History teacher sure can write!

I have read Mr. Dunphey's letter six times.

I have looked up words from the letter.

Iniquity: Lack of justice, wicked.

Immoral: Violating principals of right and wrong.

Scourge: A source of criticism. A whip used to inflict punishment.

Sunday, February 27, 1955
Diary Book,

The evil words from Mr. Dunphey's letter have come to pass. And more words, too — H words.

Some bad.

Some good.

This was a day of Hatred. Horror. Help. Hope.

Morning light came slow. Had the sun forgotten it was time to rise? Had she slept past the in-between? Where was dawn?

The sky was an iron blanket. Dark. Cold.

It was black outside when we prepared to leave for church. And so quiet.

Mama and Daddy drank dark coffee. Goober had grown used to oatmeal with cider instead of milk. For me, toast with Crisco and salt, not butter.

Goober was first on the porch. First to see the Horror.

The streetlamp's light had brought the ugly sight into view.

Goober spotted the pail set at the edge of our porch, near the post by the porch steps.

"A bucket of milk, Dawnie. A big bucket," he observed.

With the way morning was still so dark, something inside held me back from wanting to see what was in that pail. But Goober was too fast. He'd already peered down in.

Goober's face was a little moon of light under the streetlamp's white. With urgency rising in him, he shouted, "Dawnie, come see!"

He was wincing. He started to cry, then wail. "Dawnie, Daddy, Mama!"

We all came at once. I was quick to see the Horror for myself.

A dead raccoon. Bloated. Belly floating up. Drowning in a bath of milk.

There was a note that said:

KILL INTEGRATION!

STOP THE DAIRY BOYCOTT!

NOW!

Daddy and Mama stood over Goober and me, blocking the streetlight, but still able to see enough to tell us to come away from the bucket.

This was the work of that strange voice calling on our telephone—*anonymous*.

This was Hatred.

My insides fought to keep down the Crisco toast. Some of it came up, but not out.

I shook and shook.

And thought of Waddle.

And worried about her being next.

I held Mama around her waist.

Buried my face in the lavender smell of Mama's church coat. Goober was shaking, too, and he buried himself into *my* coat, wetting its wool with all his crying.

I managed to tell Mama and Daddy about the man's voice on the phone, about the "milk bath" warning.

"I should have told," I cried. "We could have stopped this somehow."

Mama just hugged me tighter. She said, "Evil is powerful, Dawnie. Even with those phone calls, we had no way of knowing *this* was on the minds of evil-hearted people."

Daddy put the creature's remains in a sack. Cleaned the bucket off our porch. He somehow got rid of it all quickly, and eased us into his truck for church. We rode through the dark-as-night morning, with Mama praying silently. Where was sunrise?

Daddy greeted Reverend Collier right away, told him about the raccoon in the pail. Word spread through our congregation before Miss Eloise even had a chance to start the choir on their opening hymn.

Rather than services, our church became a stew pot of debate. People all talking at once about nonviolence, and boycotting, and integration.

Some agreeing. Some arguing. All of us angry.

I was so rattled, I couldn't hardly breathe. I couldn't hardly see, either. Even with the lights on overhead, our church seemed darker than usual. And there was so much wet blurring anything in front of my eyes.

Daylight finally came. Gray as lint.

Lady Sun had taken the day off. Maybe she was too scared to come out. Too sad to show.

Reverend Collier said, "Now is the time to act for our greatest good. The Lord has given us this day to come together."

Some people wanted to hurt Mr. Sutter and his team of milkmen. Others said we should storm his dairy.

There were people who recalled the words of Martin Luther King, Jr. They wanted only peace.

There was so much arguing. It made my stomach more queasy.

Reverend Collier had to work hard to settle his parishioners. "We must act as brothers and sisters," he said.

When the congregation had quieted down, there was one thing everyone in that church agreed on — this was a time for light and prayer.

And Help. And Healing for me and my family.

Miss Nora handed out candles. She lit hers first, then touched its tiny flame to Roger's candle, who put his to Yolanda's. It went from there, flicker to flicker, bright to brighter, until our church glowed on this gray morning.

Everyone gathered in a circle around me, Mama, Goober, and Daddy.

Miss Eloise took it from there. She didn't need her organ. She just started singing:

> *Believe in the light of the Lord*
> *Feel his goodness*
> *Know his strength*
> *Let him lead us on this day*
> *Faith, strong, faith*
> *Is the shepherd's way.*

That music was as warm and as bright as the shine of so many candles. The power of our voices filled our rickety church.

Filled me, too.

With Hope.

Monday, February 28, 1955
Diary Book,

Mr. Dunphey is gone!

We were told today that he's chosen to go back to Boston. But how could he choose that so fast?

I don't think Mr. Dunphey *chose* that. I think it was *chosen* for him. In the lunchroom, I heard some of the other kids calling Mr. Dunphey

"Mr. Dummy." They say he cooked his own goose. They say our new teacher, Mrs. Harris, has been teaching at Prettyman forever, and that she knows the real truth about American history.

At supper when I told Mama and Daddy about all of this, Daddy shook his head. "A shame," he said.

Goober repeated, "Shame, shame, shame."

Dear Mr. Dunphey,
   I hope wherever you are, it is far away from the scourge of racial hatred. I hope there are no iniquities in Boston. I miss you.
                              Yours truly,
                              Dawnie Rae Johnson,
                              Prettyman Coburn, 7th Grade

Tuesday, March 1, 1955
Diary Book,

Can't write long. I've fallen very behind on my schoolwork. Mrs. Elmer's letting me make up the Biology test tomorrow. (Well—at least she says it'll be tomorrow. I learned my lesson from last time—Mrs. Elmer has a tricky memory.)

I also missed Math and English.

Unless some miracle happens, I have no chance of earning my way to being Bell Ringer.

If I were allowed to attend Study Hall, I'd be able to catch up. Today I banged the erasers harder than hard. Stomped my feet, too.

Later

There was one good thing about today. Spring training has begun for Major League Baseball. That means Jackie's got his bat hiked high, getting ready to play. Yay, Jackie, yay!

Wednesday, March 2, 1955
Diary Book,

I took the Biology test today. At least Mrs. Elmer gave the test when she said she'd give the test. But man sakes, that test tripped me up. I got confused about the parts of a cell—nucleus, cell wall, flagella. Which is the outer layer? I couldn't remember, even though I'd studied hard. The stuff about bacteria came to me a little easier.

We got a story assigned for English class— "The Three Questions" by Leo Tolstoy.

Here are three questions by Dawnie Rae Johnson:

1. Why is school so hard for me now?
2. When will my eraser-clapping torture end?
3. What really happened to Mr. Dunphey?

Later

Mama and Daddy were glued to the radio tonight. They'd turned the volume up, which always means there's something they especially want to hear.

I listened close when I heard the man on the radio say, "It's yet to be determined if the child has sustained injuries."

There was a news report about a Negro girl named Claudette Colvin. Today she refused to give up her seat on a bus in Montgomery, Alabama, to a white woman after the driver demanded it.

Claudette was carried off the bus backward, while being kicked and handcuffed on her way to the police station.

Dear Claudette Colvin,

I know how scared you were on that segregated bus. I know how you felt when the driver demanded that you move, and all of a sudden you were carried backward.

You wanted to kick those people back, didn't you? I know.

Love,
Dawnie Rae

Thursday, March 3, 1955
Diary Book,

Less than two months till May. If anybody asks who's counting, I will be quick to tell them—I've got ten fingers and ten toes, and I have used each and every one five times over to tick off the days till I can break free on my pogo.

Friday, March 4, 1955
Diary Book,

My report card came today. My grades have slipped. Being sick and missing school set me back. I got all Bs. Not a single A!

I did not make the honor roll. My name will not be in the newspapers near Gertie's, whose name will be at the top of the list of students with last names beginning with the letter *F.*

Saturday, March 5, 1955
Diary Book,

There's one thing integration has not put a halt to, and that's Mama's laundry business. I guess no matter who goes to school with who, people still like their collars and cuffs done right. Daddy was right. People know a good thing when it's good. And Mama's way of doing laundry is the best.

It seems the more laundry Mama takes in, the more requests she gets. Her reputation is growing. Daddy's put together a system for getting it all done.

Mama washes and presses. Daddy folds, then wraps the clean items in their brown delivery paper. I label the packages with the names of each one's owner. Goober stacks them. This is how we spend Saturdays, and many weekday evenings after homework and supper.

Daddy's taken to making the laundry deliveries in his truck. Something's changed in Daddy. He's stopped calling laundry women's work.

Today Daddy told Mama, "You oughta hang out a shingle, Loretta."

"What kind of *shingle*?" Mama was only paying attention partway. She was pressing a collar tip with the nose of her iron.

"You need a sign outside that says 'Loretta's Laundry.'" Daddy seemed to be thinking hard on his suggestion.

Mama didn't look up from her ironing board. "Who'll see my *shingle*?"

"Your customers," Daddy said.

"My *customers* are all from Ivoryton. They won't come close to this neighborhood. *I* go to *them*, remember?"

Daddy was lining up the corners on a pillowcase, preparing to fold it.

Steam rose from Mama's iron. Her face glistened from its heat. She said, "There is not a single one of those people who will come to this neighborhood, Curtis, not even to drop off or pick up their own clothes. Expecting *them* to come to *me* is expecting cats to play peacefully with dogs. It'll never happen."

Daddy didn't press the issue, but I could tell by the determined way he was folding the pillowcase that the discussion wasn't over.

Mama didn't let it go. She shook her head. "It'll be a long day off before anybody from Ivoryton comes to see my *shingle*."

Sunday, March 6, 1955
Diary Book,

March is coming in with a roar. It snowed today, then turned to rain, then got icy. This is not like Virginia. Hurry up, spring! My pogo stick's waiting.

Monday, March 7, 1955
Diary Book,

I've thought of a way to make the clapping of erasers go faster, and that's to sing while clapping them.

But what song goes well with erasers? I need something with a sure rhythm.

When I told Mr. Williams my idea, he said, "Singing *does* make unpleasant work tolerable." He told me to sing "This Little Light of Mine," one of my favorite songs from church.

The clapping did go faster, but it's very hard to shine though a cloud of chalk dust. And that white stuff still clings to my clothes and hair, and the insides of my nose.

Tuesday, March 8, 1955
Diary Book,

Do teachers even talk to each other? Don't they know they're each assigning a bundle of homework to the same students at the same time? I can *do* the work, but it's getting *all* the work done on time that's twisting me up.

Everything's due next Friday! Everything!

Tonight I read and read and read Leo Tolstoy's "The Three Questions" for English class. Then, for Biology, I read and read and read about something called "cell division." History has not been the same since Mr. Dunphey left. We don't *talk* about things in class. We read, Mrs. Harris tells us what she thinks about what we've read, then there's a quiz.

So, tonight, I read and read and read about the Virginia Plan of 1787, and memorized stuff about how this plan helped develop the branches of government.

Then on a Math worksheet I wrote and wrote and wrote answers to a whole mess of questions about exponents.

When my eyes broke free from crossing, I went back to my Biology book, and read, for fun, about froggy innards.

Thursday, March 10, 1955
Diary Book,

There was an assembly at school today. Mr. Lloyd, the principal, announced the arrival of what will be called "The Prettyman Bell." He held up a picture of The Prettyman Bell, which is set to be delivered to our school in May.

Mr. Lloyd said the new Bell Ringer will be announced at that time.

This afternoon, as I clapped and clapped those erasers clean, I heard that bell sounding in my thoughts.

Saturday, March 12, 1955
Diary Book,

Mr. Sutter came calling again. It was morning this time. He was holding a small crate in both his arms. Daddy greeted him. I was in our side yard, working on my batter's swing, slicing through this cold day with the weight of my bat's wood. Daddy didn't see me, but I had a good view of him from behind.

Mr. Sutter said, "Curtis, I'm here to offer you your job back. This boycott has been hard on all of us. To be honest, my business has taken a real dip with so many Negroes not purchasing my products. The boycott has spread from Hadley to towns all over. Not one colored customer or supplier will buy from me. If things don't pick up, I'm at risk of having to shut down."

Mr. Sutter held out the crate toward Daddy. He said, "I've brought you and your family some cheese, and our best butter — Sutter's Premium Salted."

I've never tasted Sutter's Premium Salted. We can't afford it.

I was glad not to be in Daddy's shoes right then. He had a hard decision to make. He wanted a job badly. But the boycott had brought on some ugly, dangerous things. And — Sutter's Premium Salted was as good as a crate filled with gold.

Daddy didn't even take a moment to think about Mr. Sutter's offer. He said, "Sir, while I'm thankful for your butter, I can't work for you. Your advertisement in our local newspaper made your opinions about segregation very clear."

There was silence between the two men. Finally Mr. Sutter said, "I acted in haste, Curtis. I didn't know where this integration was going. Besides, that was in the past. Can we just move on?"

There was pleading in Mr. Sutter's voice. He was near to begging.

Daddy said, "I've moved on, sir."

The straightforward way Daddy spoke is not how Negroes talk to whites in Hadley. Daddy was polite, but he was also standing up to Mr. Sutter.

Daddy said, "Thank you for the offer, but my answer is no." Mr. Sutter couldn't say anything to that.

He set the crate on our porch steps. He was leaving Daddy his gift. Daddy shook his head. He lifted the crate, handed it back to Mr. Sutter. "No, thank you, sir."

Sunday, March 13, 1955
Diary Book,

I don't know if Mama's requests for laundry have doubled, or if the same number of people are sending more clothes to be cleaned and pressed. But man sakes, have the piles grown! On Sundays we no longer linger after church services for doughnuts and fellowship. We come right home and get to laundering.

Today I asked Mama, "Isn't Sunday the day the Lord made for resting?"

Mama said, "If the Lord had meant us to rest, he wouldn't have blessed us with so many shirts and skirts that need cleaning and pressing."

Lord, I'm tired of laundry!

Monday, March 14, 1955
Early Morning

Dear Month of March,

Please make up your mind! You seem very confused about who you want to be—winter or spring. Today you threw down more snow, enough to make Hadley look like a Northern town in December.

March, the official first day of spring is around the corner, so can you please go more in that direction?

It's hard to be in-between, I know. I was born when it was part night, part day, so I understand having a toe in both places. I wake up during the in-between, so I know what it's like to have one eye looking ahead and the other glancing back.

With me going to Prettyman, I'm between a colored world and a white one, so I feel the struggle of being pulled two opposite ways at the same time.

But March, I'm depending on you. In case you forgot, spring is not cold. Spring has no snow. Please be spring.

Begging,
Dawnie Rae Ready-for-a-
Warm-Day Johnson

Later

As sick as I am of winter weather, there was one good thing about today's cold. After school, Gertie and me stopped at Orem's Pasture on the way home, where we made good use of the snow.

It was Gertie's idea.

"Dawnie," she asked, "why are there only snow-*men*, and not snow ladies?"

I hadn't ever thought about it, but Gertie was right. The closest I'd ever seen to a snow *lady* was a snow angel, but who knew if they were boys or girls.

Before I could answer, Gertie was rolling and packing snow to make a snow lady's body.

"Do the middle," she encouraged, so I started gathering enough snow for the tummy of our lady.

We formed the head together, placing it on top of the body's two parts.

"Now we make it a *her*," Gertie said.

Gertie had a pocketful of more gumdrops and licorice. She handed me a bundle of drops. I got right to work on a face. This snow lady would be colorful — orange eyes, a grape gumdrop nose. Gertie made the snow lady's mouth, a wide smile, made bright from red-licorice lips.

Gertie bumped her boot to mine. She said, "Dawnie, you're good with gumdrops."

"You got a way with licorice, Gertie," I said.

Gertie put her arm around both my shoulders. She led me to stepping back away from our snow creation so we could see it better from a ways off.

"Our snow lady needs to be more fancy," Gertie said.

Gertie decorated the sides of the lady's snow-ball head with lemon gumdrops to form loop earrings. The gumdrop jewels caught glints of the afternoon sun.

With two fallen twigs, I positioned snow lady arms that reached up toward the cloudless sky.

"That's a happy lady," Gertie said.

With all those gumdrop colors, our snow lady did look good. Gertie bit off a piece of licorice she'd yanked from her pocket. She chewed slowly. She was eyeing our creation, and thinking. Gertie snapped her licorice in two, shared a piece with me. Finally she said, "Our lady needs a stole."

At first I thought Gertie was talking about something having to do with *stealing*, until she explained that a *stole* is like a mink collar a grown-up wears for going to the theater.

"Like to the movies?" I asked.

"Like to a Broadway show or the opera," Gertie said.

For me, ladies with fur collars going to the opera was stuff that only *happened* in movies.

"Have *you* ever been to a Broadway show or the opera?" I asked.

"Once — to each."

"Is it like going to a baseball game at a stadium?"

"Baseball at a stadium is much better," Gertie said.

"Do ladies wear *stoles* to a stadium?" I had to know these things.

"The ones with the seats close-up do," said Gertie.

Gertie volunteered her scarf for our snow lady's stole. She draped it from the back of the snow lady, coming around to hang off each of her twiggy arms.

"That looks silly," I said.

"Lady clothes can be that way," said Gertie. "But it'll let people know this is no snow*man* — it's a snow *lady* who's going places."

Since Gertie had given up her scarf, I let our snow lady have my mittens. I figured March would make up its mind soon enough, and decide to become spring. So I was happy to give up my mittens.

Gertie was quick to share one of her mittens with me. "You take my other one." She fitted her left mitten onto my bare hand, kept the right mitten for herself. Then Gertie pulled open her coat pocket, still filled with candy. "Put your other hand in here to keep it warm," she encouraged.

I slid my hand down in. The gumdrops and licorice twigs greeted my fingers.

My coat had a pocket, too. "Put *your* free hand in here," I told Gertie.

Gertie did the same as me, slid her hand down in my coat pocket.

We said good-bye to Hadley's first-ever snow lady. We walked the rest of the way, toward our neighborhood, with warm hands. Each wearing one mitten, the other hand safe in the pocket of a friend.

Gertie had taught me something important, too. When I do get to a stadium to watch Jackie Robinson steal bases, I will need to wear a *stole*.

Wednesday, March 16, 1955
Diary Book,

Tonight Daddy helped me with my homework by reading Leo Tolstoy's "The Three Questions" out loud. It's a fable about a king who wants to find answers to the three most important questions in life.

Before kissing me good night, Daddy asked me the study guide questions from the story.

1. What is the best time to do each thing?
2. Who are the most important people to work with?
3. What is the most important thing to do at all times?

Here's what I told Daddy.

1. The *best* time to do each thing is when you're sure it's the *right* time.
2. The most important people to work with are people who need your help.
3. The most important thing to do at all times is the thing that helps those people.

Daddy said, "You, Dawnie Rae, have the right answers to 'The Three Questions.'"

Friday, March 18, 1955
Diary Book,

I showed Mr. Williams the story by Leo Tolstoy. I watched his face as he read it. His eyes worked smoothly across the pages, taking in each word, pausing some, thinking.

He answered the three questions this way:

1. Yesterday is past — forget it. Tomorrow is the future — don't fret it. Today is a gift, and that's why it's called the present. The best time to do each thing is now.
2. The most important people are the ones God's put right in front of you. Treat them like you want to be treated.
3. The most important thing to do at all times is to believe.

I said, "You, Mr. Williams, have the right answers to 'The Three Questions.'"

Monday, March 21, 1955
Diary Book,

Today is the first official day of spring, but there is nothing spring-y about it. Our front lawn is crunchy from icy dew that won't let go. And it's cold outside. I refuse to wear my hood, even though I still need it. Who wears a hood in March? Not me.

Saturday, March 26, 1955
Diary Book,

Daddy drove all the way to Norfolk looking for a job. He was gone for two days. He returned early this morning, honking his horn loudly as he pulled up to our house in his truck. Mama came out in her house dress. Goober and I followed in our pajamas. I was certain Daddy'd gotten a job. Why else would he be pressing his horn to make such happy sounds?

Morning was the color of a pearl. As soon as we got onto our doorstep, I saw why Daddy was honking. On each side of his truck he'd had a sign painted in curly letters:

LORETTA'S LAUNDRY. FULL SERVICE. FREE DELIVERY.

He said to Mama, "I hope you'll hire a man whose child is taking such a bold stand by integrating her school."

Mama had picked the morning paper up off our doorstep.

"Look, Dawnie!" Goober said. "Do you see Daddy's truck?"

I smiled bigger than big. "I see it, Goob. I see it!"

Daddy came to where we stood. He hugged Mama. "Can I start calling you 'boss'?"

Mama gave the top of Daddy's head a playful slap with the folded newspaper.

She said, "You're hired."

Tuesday, March 29, 1955
Diary Book,

Daddy's truck is drawing a lot of attention. Loretta's Laundry has officially come to Hadley, Virginia.

Thursday, March 31, 1955
Diary Book,

Mrs. Taylor told us today that the Bell Ringer job will now be decided by the results of something called the "Seventh-Grade All Competency Exam." Each student will take a final test for the school year. The test will cover every subject.

So, I need to know everything about parts of a cell. And, there might be so many questions about branches of government I'll be wishing those branches could help me climb a tree out of my classroom window. And I bet the test will have enough algorithms to stuff a sofa. And probably *thirty* questions about "The Three Questions."

The test will determine who becomes Bell Ringer starting in May and continuing through the next school year.

Later

Tonight when I helped Mama pack up laundry deliveries for Daddy to make tomorrow, I told Mama and Daddy about the Seventh-Grade All Competency Exam. Mama set her iron on its holder. The iron's steam sputtered from its spout.

"*One* test decides? Whose knuckleheaded idea was that?" Mama asked.

"The school's," I said.

Daddy was balancing a stack of brown-paper laundry packages. His chin secured the one on top. "There's a gift in it, Dawnie," he said with a voice that knows.

A giant exam. Where's the gift in that?

Friday, April 1, 1955
Diary Book.

The man on the radio announced the official start of baseball season is only ten days away! And even though it's the first day of April, this is no April Fool's joke. Batting time is finally coming soon.

The announcer asked everybody who was listening, "Will the Brooklyn Dodgers win the world championship?"

Daddy said, "If Jackie Robinson has anything to do with it, they will."

The Dodgers have come close a few times, with Jackie playing on their team. They've played in seven World Series games, but not once in any of those series have they won the world championship.

Dear Mr. Jackie Robinson,
   Will the Brooklyn Dodgers make it to the World Series?
   I want to know.

Wednesday, April 6, 1955
Diary Book.

Thunder. Lightning. Rain. Rain. Raaaain.

I am not like most people when it comes to a storm. I like the rain and everything it makes. When the sky sends down a sprinkle, I pray for a sheet. Raindrops on my face make me happy. And, I'm a true puddle lover.

When there's so much thunder that it sounds like heaven has spilled a bag of baseballs, I ask the Lord to have someone up there hire a drum band to bring on more booming.

As for lightning, let it strike!

How else can we see the sky's design?

Mama practically sealed me in wax paper to make sure that not a drop of wet touched my skin. And she armed me and Daddy with umbrellas as wide as our porch roof. If there was such a thing as a wet-weather mask, Mama would have insisted on one of them, too.

Today, when Daddy walked me to school, I said, "I bet you can't make it to Waverly and Vine without wanting to open your umbrella."

"Bet," Daddy said.

We were already soaked, and Daddy didn't look too pleased. But Daddy, he's a smarty. He slid his newspaper out from his coat's inside pocket, opened it wide, and walked under the tent made by its pages. As good as rain feels on my face, it doesn't compare to sharing a newspaper with my daddy.

Friday, April 8, 1955
Diary Book,

More rain.

More puddles.

Goody, goody!

Saturday, April 9, 1955
Diary Book,

Today after delivering laundry packages, Daddy took me to the only public place in town that's not segregated — the Hadley Public Library — so I could study for the Seventh-Grade All Competency Exam.

When I got to the library, Daddy and I slid into one of the study carrels, where we laid out all my schoolbooks and papers. The library is supposed to be a quiet place, but there's one person whose whisper is loud — Gertie. She and *her* daddy were in the study carrel next to ours. They were doing the same thing, studying for the exam. As soon as I heard Gertie's voice, I folded myself over the top of my carrel, peered down, and saw Gertie's head. There aren't many people I can recognize by looking at their scalps, but from watching Gertie somersault, I know the top of her head as good as I know my own.

"Gertie!" I tried to speak softly, but it came out loud.

When Gertie looked up and saw me half climbing into her carrel, she was through with whispering. "Dawnie, come down from there. Help me study! What does *metamorphosis* mean?" she asked.

I came around to where Gertie was sitting. Daddy followed. Our fathers introduced themselves. Gertie's daddy is a small man with a kind face and glasses that slide to where his nose almost ends. When he shook Daddy's hand, he did it with both his hands wrapped around Daddy's. He introduced himself as Dr. Saul Feldman.

"Pleased to meet you," Daddy said, and brought his second hand around to join both the hands of Dr. Feldman.

This is another thing I will never forget if I live to be a hundred. Four hands — my daddy's strong brown ones and Dr. Feldman's gentle white ones — clasped together, greeting each other.

Dr. Feldman said to Daddy, "You have quite a daughter. Gertie's told me about Dawnie." He smiled when he said this.

We all moved to one of the library's center tables, out in the open, which we covered with our schoolbooks, papers, pencils, writing tablets, and plenty of scrap paper for figuring. We started with Gertie's science question.

What is metamorphosis?

I knew the answer right off.

"It's when something changes from one thing into another."

Sunday, April 10, 1955
Diary Book,

I don't believe in the Easter Bunny, but I do believe in sweet things and surprises. Today, Easter Sunday, I got both.

At church, Yolanda kept to herself during the service. But afterward, when it was time for fellowshipping, Yolanda asked if I wanted to play "Tell the Truth or Die Tryin'." She was making an X over her heart before I even said yes.

Yolanda started off the game. "Cross my heart, hope to die. Stick a needle in my eye. If I'm lyin', watch me cryin'. 'Cause I know I will be dyin'."

We pressed our foreheads together. Neither one of us had shed a "lyin' cryin' dyin'" tear.

"Dawnie," Yolanda said quietly, "I'm gonna tell you something that's the truth, but you gotta promise to keep it between us."

I said, "Cross my heart, hope to die. Stick a needle in my eye."

Yolanda took a breath. She lowered her voice even more. "I wish I could go with you to Prettyman Coburn," she admitted. "I want shiny books, and classes with names of things that sound like they make you smarter just by saying them. Most of all, I want to be in school together, Dawnie."

266

Yolanda hooked her pinkie to mine. She said, "I know it's hard being the only Negro student at that school. But if I was there with you, you wouldn't be alone, and maybe we could help each other."

I locked our pinkies even tighter. "Prettyman would be a lot nicer with you in it," I said.

Yolanda said, "I'm sorry for calling you uppity, Dawnie."

I asked, "Did you hear what Reverend Collier said this morning during his sermon?"

Yolanda shook her head. "I was too busy thinking about truth tellin'."

I said, "Reverend Collier told us that Easter is about celebrating a new beginning that's come out of a dark time."

Yolanda nodded.

"Let's go to the fellowship table and get us some colored eggs," I said.

"Nice making up with you," said Yolanda. She pressed her forehead to mine for the second time. "And that's the truth."

Monday, April 11, 1955
Diary Book,

Gertie knows everything there is to know about government and the Virginia Plan of 1787, and how a bill becomes a law, and what statutes are.

No doubt she will ace the questions about American history.

I asked Gertie, "How badly do you want to be Bell Ringer?"

"Not half as bad as you."

"Are you worried about the exam?" I asked.

Gertie was at it again, giving the same answer for a different question. "Not half as bad as you."

Then she added, "As long as they don't make me sponge the blackboard and clap erasers."

Like Gertie, I repeated the answer, but put the answer onto myself. I said, "As long as they don't make *me* sponge the blackboard and clap erasers."

Tuesday, April 12, 1955
Diary Book,

The afternoon's drizzle is as thick as blackstrap, the same molasses that once filled my lunch tin.

I should be studying, but my mind is someplace far away, daydreaming about diamonds.

Diamonds with bases for running and rounding, and pretending to be player number 42 — Jackie Robinson.

If I had more time to go out and play, I bet I could hit an A+ home run on the Seventh-Grade All Competency Exam.

Wednesday, April 13, 1955
Diary Book,

I thought the rain had stopped, but it's back with an attitude.

As much as I love rain, I've now had enough of it.

Rain, rain, go away.

Come again some other day.

Stay all gone so I can play (after I get through seventh grade).

Thursday, April 21, 1955
Diary Book,

I've missed you! I thought you got lost somehow. But today I found out where you've been. Goober got his hands on you. He's kept you from me, and for this whole week he's made you *his* Diary Book. Eight full days without writing, eight days of wondering where you were, has been as hard as all these months with no pogo stick and a snowed-on, rained-on tree mop. There's some stuff to catch up on, but I'm pressed for time. The Seventh-Grade All Competency Exam is next week. If I don't write about what's happened, though, I'm gonna pop.

Your pages are scribbled and drawn on, and a mess. Goober's covered you with pictures of pogo sticks and peanuts, peanuts, peanuts!! Peanuts with faces and arms and legs.

And to make it worse, I'm now running out of pages for writing. I probably won't make it till summer with the few pages left. Summer's the best time for a diary, because I'll *have* time to write.

I AM SO ANGRY AT GOOBER!! And I told him so, too. I hollered at him as soon as I found my scribbled-on Diary Book's pages, where Goober'd left the book on my bed. I don't care that my hollering made him cry and rock. I don't care that Goober told me he didn't mean to ruin my book's pages, and that he just wanted to draw stuff! I don't care one bit! Goober has broken Daddy's rule about keeping your hands to yourself!! First my pogo stick, now this.

Goober ruins everything!

How come I got Goober for a brother?

How come Goober's so . . . so . . . ugh!

How come Goober's Goober?

I'm too angry for more catching up. If I write anything else, my pencil will snap. That's how mad I am!

I'm going outside to slam my bat at the tree mop. I don't care that it's raining knives and forks. *I'm* raining knives and forks!!!

Friday, April 22, 1955
Diary Book,

The new hiding place for my diary is in my shoe box, where the Vaselines once lived, where that frog almost lost his life in the name of science, and where I've hidden my Christmas money. Goober can't find my Diary Book there.

I've now had the chance to look more closely at Goober's scribbles. His peanut people have broken legs and arms. And heads split open. And bandaged noses. And smiles turned down. And Xs for eyes.

Goober's labeled each broken peanut person. He's named all of them after himself.

Saturday, April 23, 1955
Diary Book,

Before Prettyman, there wasn't a single lesson, paper, assignment, or test that turned me to gooseflesh. Now I'm *all* goose. Nervous as a jumpy bird.

Back at Bethune when I took that test with Yolanda and Roger, I didn't know what to expect, so I didn't study. I was only just a little nervous. But that was different. The only truth *that* test *unveiled* is that it's no secret I've got what it takes to succeed at Prettyman. But do I have enough smarts to pass Prettyman's Seventh-Grade All Competency Exam?

Sunday, April 24, 1955
Diary Book,

Today was a church service filled with good surprises.

That preacher from Alabama, Martin Luther King, Jr., had come back to Shepherd's Way as our guest. Martin talked about the Sutter's Dairy boycott.

He spoke about our progress as a people, and told us that change takes time. Nobody argued about nonviolence. But plenty grumbled about non-buttered toast, no milk for coffee, and baking without cream.

Before the protests got out of hand, Reverend Collier introduced a new member of Shepherd's

Way. "Brother Arne Pelham, welcome."

A pudgy man stood and nodded to the congregation. The reverend asked Mr. Pelham to tell us about himself. But Reverend Collier didn't give Mr. Pelham time to speak. The reverend was eager to share the good news.

"Brother Pelham is a dairy supplier who's come to Hadley from Maryland. His company, Pelham Dairy, will start operation throughout Lee County this month."

I tugged at Daddy. "What does that mean?"

"It means we can buy our milk from Brother Pelham," Daddy explained. "We now have a Negro selling us dairy products."

"Will there be a Negro milkman, too?"

Daddy nodded.

Mr. Pelham was glad to shake some hands.

Reverend Collier then introduced another church visitor. He motioned to the back of the church, encouraging the guest to come forward.

It was Mr. Dunphey!

He stepped to the pulpit and stood next to Reverend Collier. I blinked to make sure I was not dreaming this up. But as soon as Mr. Dunphey told us about being a teacher at Prettyman, and writing the letter to the newspaper, and believing in change, I knew this was no dream — I was wide awake.

My heart's *beat-beat-beat* proved I was far from asleep.

Mr. Dunphey told the congregation about being asked by Mr. Lloyd, our school principal, to leave Prettyman. And he told us about going back to Boston, but thinking twice on it.

"Change starts with one person, then another, then more. I'm only one man, but progress can start with me, and with each of us."

Mr. Dunphey's words got some people to clap.

He said, "School administrators can kick me out of Prettyman, but nobody can make me leave Hadley."

Reverend Collier said, "Brother Dunphey, you are a shepherd for peace."

And there it was, another *H* word at our church — *Happy*!

Later

At home, I showed Mama and Daddy the scribbles and pictures Goober had made in this diary book.

A sharp frown pinched at Mama's face. Daddy's, too.

Daddy went to his truck and came back with a roll of brown paper used to wrap laundry packages. He pulled out two long sheets, spread each on the floor of our living room.

"Goober, Dawnie," he called. "We've got work to do."

I was not in the mood for chores. Or folding linens. Or hanging shirts to dry.

Daddy instructed us to each lie flat, faceup, on one of the paper sheets. I looked at Mama, then Goober. They were as puzzled as me.

"Be still," Daddy said. "Goober's first."

Daddy pressed Goober's open hands flat down on the paper, and pulled his arms away from his sides. With Mama's laundry pencil, he traced Goober's outline — head, neck, arms, legs, hands, and each finger. Goober started to giggle, then wriggle. "Daddy, you're tickling me."

I was next — head, arms, neck, legs, and the outline of my hair. Goober was right. It did tickle.

Mama watched, and knew just what to do next. She taped the tracings to our living room's biggest wall. She printed our names on the bottom.

She handed me and Goober each a laundry pencil. "Write *good* words. Draw *nice* pictures," Mama instructed.

Goober and me, we didn't waste any time.

On the inside of my silhouette I wrote: "SMART. BRAVE. INTENTION. POGO. HOME RUN."

I drew baseballs and frogs and bells and lots of 42s, Jackie Robinson's jersey number.

Goober's pencil got busy, too.

He wrote: "GOOBER. BOY. ME. FREE. RUN. FLY."

His drawings covered the whole page, inside the tracing and out.

He drew dancing peanuts, smiling peanuts, peanuts playing in leaves, and peanuts with wings.

When we were done, Mama said to Daddy, "Curtis, I will never badger you again about hanging wallpaper in our living room. We now have the prettiest walls on Marietta Street."

Monday, April 25, 1955
Diary Book,

We got our first delivery from Pelham's Dairy today. That milk tasted real good with my buttered toast.

Tonight Mama made me a warm cup of milk before bed to help me sleep before the exam. But as welcome as that warm milk was, I can't sleep.

I'm writing during the black-night hours that churn slowly before the in-between. For three nights in a row, sleep has not been my friend. Two days till the exam.

It's *still* raining, but less.

Tuesday, April 26, 1955
Diary Book,

Can you cram for an exam?

Can you scram from an exam?

Is there ham at an exam?

I'm getting punchy!!

Wednesday, April 27, 1955
Diary Book,

Today was the Seventh-Grade All Competency Exam. The rain had stopped, but there was wet everywhere. I'm sure Bethune's red bricks have stained the streets. After days of downpour, that school is probably a puddle of mud.

The air was thicker than biscuit gravy this morning. Mrs. Taylor had opened our classroom windows. No breeze came. Just heaviness everywhere. Mama made me wear galoshes to school. If there's one thing that makes your feet sweat, it's galoshes. And the one thing that makes the rest of you sweat is sweaty feet.

Mrs. Taylor handed out each test packet, face-down. She looked at the wall clock. "Students, begin," she said. I flipped my test packet over faster than a spatula flips a burnt pancake. At the top of my test it said *Science for the Ages*, the name of my Biology textbook. Daddy had been right. Here was my gift.

The first section of my test was all about the dead frog! I had to draw its innards and explain how they work. So, I was starting off the exam with real good thoughts in my mind. That set the tone for the rest of the test. *Real good.*

I set my pencil to work, labeling the frog's stomach, liver, and heart.

My own heart was beating a happy dance of relief. Not once did I need to use my pencil eraser. I was sure of my answers. By the time I got to the parts of the test that had to do with government and algorithms, I was warmed up and feeling fine.

The questions about "The Three Questions" didn't stop me one bit. By now, me and Mr. Tolstoy were buddies.

When I was done, I reviewed my work. I put down my pencil. I watched the minute hand rise on the clock. I'd finished with two minutes left to flex my sweaty toes.

Later

The exam is over. Even with the gift that came in getting a test that started off with frog dissection, I feel like *I've* been dissected. Oh, my innards!

Thursday, April 28, 1955
Diary Book,

Gertie was glad for so many exam questions about democracy and the branches of American government.

"Easy, easy, pillow squeezy" was how she described her test.

I'm just glad Gertie's got know-how about branches, and I've got a brain for frog's legs.

Now we wait. For our grades.

Friday, April 29, 1955
Diary Book,

Sunshine!

At last.

Warm sunshine.

Happy sunshine.

Shine on, sunshine!

Saturday, April 30, 1955
Diary Book,

My tree mop is worn from the winter weather. But with so much sun, its ropes are dry and dangling.

The mop is as stringy as ever, and ready to play.

This afternoon I reared back with my bat, swinging righty, then met the mop — *bam!* — and sent it soaring.

If that mop could sing, it would have joined me for a chorus of "Welcome Spring."

Sunday, May 1, 1955
Diary Book,

I asked Mama if I could please get my pogo stick out from the cellar. "Patience, Dawnie" was all she said.

That means no.

Monday, May 2, 1955
Diary Book,

Before now, I never gave the first days of May a second thought other than to mark the beginning of my birthday month. But this is May with a capital *M*.

I was awake before the dew even knew what to do. With Daddy now working for Mama, he drove me to Ivoryton, let me out at Waverly Street, where we usually part ways on foot.

Waddle greeted me this morning! The markings on her face were the same, but she looked different somehow, smaller. She was partway under a rosebush, scuttling back to where I couldn't see, out again to greet me, then back to hiding.

Mrs. Thompson's rosebush was beginning to shed its winter brown. There were no blooms yet, but come summer, pink buds will bring joy.

I followed Waddle to the spot under the bush. I pulled back the low parts of green. Waddle's whiskers twitched.

She had four baby raccoons suckling her!

They were tiny as newborn kittens, and just as hungry. None of them had face masks or tail rings. Just fur, and tightly shut eyes.

I whispered, "Waddle, you're a ma! You're a beautiful ma!"

I left Waddle to her babies, letting a small singsong fill my thoughts:

Waddle's a ma . . . Waddle's a ma . . .

When I got to the front of the school building, the new bell was there, but was covered in what looked like blue silk.

The Prettyman Bell was waiting for its unveiling.

The entire school gathered, with seventh graders standing in a row closest to Mr. Lloyd.

Mr. Lloyd spoke into a megaphone. "This bell will serve as a salutation to all who enter Prettyman Coburn School each morning. And the bell will usher students out in the afternoon. The power of its sound will be in the hands of our new Bell Ringer."

Gertie nudged me.

Mr. Lloyd continued. "Our seventh-grade class has the Bell Ringer privilege beginning this month, and extending through the 1955–1956 school year."

I wanted Mr. Lloyd to stop talking. I was eager to see the Prettyman Bell. But Mr. Lloyd, he sure was taking pride in his megaphone.

"As our seventh-grade teachers tally test scores, the question remains — who will the Bell Ringer be?"

Quietly, with my lips making the words, I prayed a silent prayer: *me, me, me.*

That's when Mr. Lloyd unveiled the Prettyman Bell. He flung off the blue silk, let it flutter behind him. That bell was as big as Goober! It was a brass dream come true, waiting proudly on iron hinges.

My prayer rose up, this time from the deep place somewhere between my heart and belly. The spot where hard wanting lives.

Me . . . me . . . me . . .

Tuesday, May 3, 1955
Diary Book,

How long does it take to grade some tests? It's been a week since we took the Seventh-Grade All Competency Exam.

The Prettyman Bell is ready for a ringer.

I'm sick and tired of clapping erasers.

I can't take another minute of Mama's fly-paper and fan.

Enough chalk dust!

Thursday, May 5, 1955
Diary Book,

Before the sun even knew it was morning, I was awake in bed. Now that spring's here, light comes sooner into my window. The in-between is the bluest blue, with silver-pink curling in at its edges.

Our whole house was asleep when I crept to the cellar to get my pogo stick. I know Mama had told me not to go near the stick until my birthday, but between *waiting* for the exam results, and *waiting* to see if I'll become the Bell Ringer, and *waiting* for me to turn thirteen—I'm *sick* of *waiting*.

I pushed past cobwebs and puddles left from so many days of rain, to the back corner of our cellar's canning closet where my pogo had been stored.

When I pulled the chain that turned on the ceiling bulb, the closet was lit, yellow, dim. There's not much to that closet. What you see, is what you see. And I could see that my pogo stick was gone! I looked under the potato bin and behind the canning shelf where Mama had stored pickles all winter. No pogo stick. Anyplace.

I couldn't help what I did next. "GOOBER!" I shouted.

Daddy and Mama came running. Daddy was holding a flashlight. Mama held Goober's hand.

I was breathing hard, like *I'd* been the one racing to the closet.

"Where's my pogo?" I hollered.

Mama said, "Where's your patience, Dawnie? You were supposed to wait until your birthday to come looking for that stick. You disobeyed me."

I kicked at the potato bin. I was thinking on what to say.

Daddy said to Mama, "Should we punish her, Loretta?"

Mama said, "Yes, Curtis, let's punish her."

Daddy told me to follow him to the subcellar, a cramped, tiny space where our house pipes live. Only the two of us could fit.

Daddy pointed the beam from his flashlight. He moved toward the direction of the light's ray, which he'd fixed to shine onto an odd shape leaning against the dirt wall. Right then, in our subcellar, Daddy *unveiled* my punishment. There was no blue silk, like the fabric that had covered the Prettyman Bell, but a burlap sheet had kept the surprise hidden—a new pogo stick! A red Ace Flyer with green tassels at the end of each handle.

Mama called, "Has she gotten her punishment?"

Daddy peered through the small opening that led up to where Mama and Goober waited. "I've socked it to her good," he said.

This is the best punishment ever!

Saturday, May 7, 1955
Diary Book.

Warm weather has a way of putting people in a good mood. Yolanda came over today. I showed her how high I could jump on my new pogo stick. Yolanda made up a rhyme, right on the spot.

That pogo stick's new, it's never been seen.
Its body is red, its tassels are green.
So much pogo joy, you won't want a breather.
That Ace Flyer doesn't squeak, either!

We giggled at the whole silly thing.

Monday, May 9, 1955
Diary Book,

I now know four things for sure about Gertie Feldman.

Gertie Feldman is the daughter of a doctor.

Gertie Feldman is smart.

Gertie Feldman is a big faker!

Gertie Feldman will be my true good friend for a long time.

Our exams came back today. I scored high, but not high enough to be named Bell Ringer. I missed two out of twenty-two questions, and lost points for misspelling *metamorphosis* and *nucleus*.

Gertie got a perfect score on her test. She gained three points for spelling everything right.

This afternoon there was another assembly,

this time to name the Bell Ringer. Mrs. Taylor made me finish clapping erasers before the gathering. When I arrived at the bell, I was covered in chalk dust, like always at that time of day. Mr. Williams, the janitor, had come with me. Miss Cora and Miss Billie, the ladies from the cafeteria, were there, too.

Mr. Lloyd's megaphone could be heard from here to Norfolk. Boy, was it loud. Mr. Lloyd called Gertie forward in front of everybody. "Now, Miss Feldman, you may christen the Prettyman Bell."

Well, it didn't take a dictionary to know what *christen* means. I've been to enough church services to know that when somebody is christened they're introduced as new and special in the eyes of God. And if the eyes of God were watching at that moment, they could see that *me, me, me* was not the one christening the Prettyman Bell.

But soon *me, me, me* saw the real and true Gertie Feldman.

As soon as Gertie curled her fingers around that bell's weighty handle, she slid her eyes toward *me, me, me*. The whole school was waiting to hear the christening of the bell. But Gertie would not oblige them. She pulled down on the bell's handle. The handle didn't budge. Then she went up on tiptoe to get her hands and the weight of her body above the handle. She tried with a will to plunge down on the handle, but it still didn't move. Not even a little bit.

Gertie gave a grunt. She bit on her bottom lip, and tried to pull the handle toward her. Still no christening. That's when I knew Gertie was faking. Someone who's so good at somersaults and talking to grown-ups could most likely ring a bell, even a big one.

Finally Gertie said, "This bell's too heavy for me. I need help."

Mr. Lloyd came forward to get the bell started, but Gertie stopped him! Before *he, he, he* could christen the bell, Gertie grabbed on to *me, me, me*!

She positioned my fingers around the bell's handle, then wrapped her hands on top of mine. The bell and its handle *were* heavy, but not heavy enough to keep Gertie from ringing it by herself.

Together we hunkered down on that handle and christened the Prettyman Bell. We sent its song right to God's ear.

But after the first strike of sound, Gertie stepped away so I could ring all by myself. And did I ever ring. The bell's handle got lighter with each yank. And as the bell started to swing on its iron hinges, its sound grew louder and louder, taking on a steady rhythm and a *claaannggg* that stirred me from the inside out.

I'm sure Mr. Lloyd didn't expect that I'd pull on that bell's handle twenty times over. But I was there to introduce that bell. Mr. Lloyd could not stop *me, me, me.*

I *claaaaannnggged* that bell for Mama and Daddy.

I *claaaaannnggged* for Jackie Robinson and Mr. Dunphey.

I *claaaaannnggged* for Mr. Williams, Miss Cora, and Miss Billie.

I pulled on that bell's handle doubly hard for Gertie and Goober, who both see things in ways others don't, and for Yolanda, who can always make me giggle.

Most of all, I christened that pretty Prettyman Bell for myself.

Dawnie Rae Johnson.

When I was done, Gertie asked Mr. Lloyd for his megaphone. He was so startled by the whole thing that he gave it to her without thinking twice.

Gertie really didn't need a megaphone. Her voice is loud enough.

She said, "I give my Bell Ringer job to Dawnie."

Not one person protested. How could they? Mr. Williams and the lunchroom ladies were clapping too loudly.

Wednesday, May 11, 1955
Diary Book,

With the school year almost over, I have a bad case of spring fever. The last day of school is this Friday.

Today Mrs. Taylor posted the roster of school jobs for next year. They were listed alphabetically, and for once my name was in the right place.

There were three names and jobs on that list that caught my eye:

Morning Salutation: Gertie Feldman
Blackboard/Erasers: Bobby Hatch
Bell Ringer: Dawnie Rae Johnson

Wednesday, May 18, 1955
Diary Book,

Happy birthday to me! I haven't written in a while, for the simple reason that this book's pages have run low because of Goober's scribbling, and I wanted to save some space for writing on my birthday.

As it turns out, I now have enough pages to

write for at least another year. I'm in bed as I fill up on writing. My red pencil is short now, but its point is still as sharp as ever.

This morning the in-between had nothing on me. I was awake while the moon started to wave good-bye. The sky was peeling open to let in the sun.

Something hard-edged poked through my pillow's softness. I knew right off what it was, and reached around to pull it out from its hiding place.

It's a new Diary Book! For my thirteenth birthday! From Goober!

I will never use the bad *H* word about my brother again. He has given me a new *H* word to describe how I feel about him. I am *humbled* by how good a soul that boy is.

My new diary has a green fabric cover and a pocket in the back. I can tell by the lavender smell coming off the book's front and by the stiff-stiff way it's been sewn together that Mama's had a hand in making it. The book has been pressed with an iron, I just know it.

The pages are the same as this diary's pages, rough at the edges from the way Goober's cut them to fit between the new book's covers. Goober's written a note on the book's inside front.

I recognize his handwriting. It says:

To Dawnie. My sister. You can fly.

Now I have reached this book's last page. It's just as well. I need to stop writing. Goober's calling me.

"Dawnie, come out and play!"

Epilogue

Dawnie returned to Prettyman Coburn School in the fall of 1955. In October of that year, the Brooklyn Dodgers won the World Series, beating the New York Yankees. It was a victory for Dodgers fans, and especially for Jackie Robinson, as this was his only championship. The World Series was a personal triumph for Dawnie, who listened to the final game of the series on the radio with her family.

The morning of October 4, 1955, marked the final World Series game. On that day, Dawnie rang the Prettyman Bell louder than ever.

Dawnie remained the only black student at Prettyman Coburn. The school was slow to integrate. Dawnie graduated from Prettyman Coburn in 1960. She was ranked third in her senior high-school class, and was the first black student to graduate from Prettyman in the school's fifty-year history. In 1963, Prettyman enrolled three more black students, but progress took time.

Dawnie won a scholarship and attended

Boston University, one of the nation's few predominantly white colleges to enroll black students at that time. She went on to receive a scholarship to Johns Hopkins University in Baltimore, where she earned her medical degree in pediatric medicine. Through her education, Dawnie learned the true nature of her brother's "special way of seeing things." Goober had what is known today as autism, a neurobiological disorder.

Dr. Dawnie Rae Johnson never married. She devoted her life's work to the advancement in understanding of neurological disorders in children. She became an active member of the NAACP.

Yolanda graduated from Bethune, also ranking high in her class. She stayed in Hadley, married a local man, and became the choir director at Shepherd's Way Baptist Church.

Dawnie's parents moved to Richmond, Virginia, the state capital. They successfully opened and operated a chain of dry-cleaning stores, called, simply, "Loretta's."

People from all over brought their clothing for laundering, tailoring, and pressing. When they picked up their items, they returned home with the cleanest, sharpest dresses and slacks in the state of Virginia.

Loretta's employed people of all races. Those who worked for Loretta's took the establishment's promise of excellence seriously. The company's most committed employee was Goober.

Gertie and Dawnie remained friends. Like Dawnie, Gertie also broke new ground at Prettyman. She was the first Jewish student to graduate.

Gertie became a labor attorney who worked on behalf of underserved Americans seeking fair employment opportunities. Soon after Gertie married in 1975, she had one child, a daughter, whom she named Dawn, after her best friend.

Women and men, who, like Dawnie, integrated their schools in the 1950s and 1960s, are still alive today, sharing their stories of triumph.

Life in America in 1954

Historical Note

At one time in America, the laws in many states kept black and white citizens separate in public places, including restaurants, movie theaters, buses, hotels, and pools. And, children of different races could not go to school together.

The laws, known as Jim Crow laws, gave school districts the legal right to keep schools racially segregated, as long as they provided an equal education to black and white students. Jim Crow laws upheld the belief that if schools were "separate but equal," it was acceptable to keep black and white students apart.

But these separate schools weren't the same. Black students were forced to work with inferior materials — shabby books, broken pencils, and facilities that needed fixing. In white public schools, students usually enjoyed new books, sports equipment, hot lunches, and extracurricular activities. Black teachers were underpaid and underrepresented among state school officials, and they struggled to get proper learning tools for their students.

The unfairness of these circumstances made black children and their parents angry. To strike out against these unjust laws, a group of African American parents from Delaware, Kansas, South Carolina, Virginia, and Washington, D.C., worked with the NAACP (National Association for the Advancement of Colored People). They sued school boards that discriminated against black children. Their case was named after Oliver Brown, one of the parents who lived in Kansas. Oliver's daughter, Linda, was prevented from attending her local all-white elementary school because she was African American.

On May 17, 1954, the Supreme Court ruled in favor of school integration in a case known as *Brown v. Board of Education of Topeka*. As part of the court's decision, it was determined that separate school facilities were not equal, and that the best way to ensure equality in education was to allow black children to enroll in any public school they wished to attend. This was not an easy fight. It took the hard work of many determined people to make school integration possible.

The *Brown v. Board of Education* ruling brought hope to students and teachers. At the same time, though, there were individuals who were strongly against school integration. Most schools did not integrate right away. Progress was slow. Many residents in Southern states resisted integration. In Southern towns, school officials upheld segregation practices, despite the law.

In September 1954, months after the *Brown v. Board of Education* decision, schools on military bases in Fort Myer and Fort Belvoir in Virginia, and Craig Air Force Base in Alabama integrated. Military base schools were required to comply immediately under federal law. Schools in Washington, D.C., also integrated.

In the state of Virginia, U.S. senator Harry F. Byrd, Sr., a segregationist, promoted a movement known as the "Southern Manifesto," which opposed integrating schools. This program was supported by more than one hundred Southern government officials. On February 25, 1956, Senator Byrd launched an initiative called the "Massive Resistance" movement that led to legislation passed in 1958 intending to prevent school integration. Massive Resistance enacted a law that cut off state funds and closed public schools that agreed to integrate. During this time, Virginia closed nine schools in four counties rather than integrate them. Virginia state courts and federal courts ruled against the Massive Resistance tactics, citing them as illegal. Schools were forced to uphold the laws set forth under the *Brown v. Board of Education* ruling.

Still, less than 2 percent of Southern schools were integrated by 1957. That year, nine African American students, known as the "Little Rock Nine," enrolled in Central High School, an all-white school in Little Rock, Arkansas. Their bravery captured the attention of Americans throughout the nation, as the violent events surrounding their attempts to enter Central High School were covered by national news media.

The same was true in 1960 when six-year-old Ruby Bridges was the first black child to attend William Frantz Elementary School, a white school in New Orleans, Louisiana.

Although these integration stories are the most well-known, many brave black children enrolled in all-white schools after integration laws were passed. Despite the taunts and abuses of segregationists, these children proceeded with strength and dignity.

School integration enraged and frightened many people, and stirred racial tensions. As a result, African American children and adults were often tormented by those who believed in segregation.

At the same time, other people stood up for what was right. They banded together and worked hard to make integration a reality.

A sign on an outhouse at a rest stop between Louisville, Kentucky, and Nashville, Tennessee, directs black patrons to the dining room behind the outhouse.

A sign reading "For Colored Only" denotes a segregated water fountain.

After the Brown v. Board of Education of Topeka *decision was reached in the U.S. Supreme Court, schools all over the nation were mandated to desegregate, and the NAACP tried to register black students in previously all-white schools throughout the South. In September of 1957 nine black students, who were chosen on the basis of their academic achievements and who would become known as the Little Rock Nine, were registered to attend Little Rock Central High School in Little Rock, Arkansas. However, after groups all over the city threatened to block the entrance to the school, the governor of Arkansas, Orval Faubus, had the Arkansas National Guard deployed to support the segregationists and keep the Little Rock Nine from entering the building. An angry mob of segregationists, who hurled physical and verbal abuse, as well as threats of lynching, and members of the Arkansas National Guard gathered on September 4, 1957, to prevent the nine students from going into the school, a move that reverberated around the nation.*

After weeks of rioting and violence, President Eisenhower, at the request of the mayor of Little Rock, Woodrow Mann, intervened and sent the 101st Airborne Division of the U.S. Army to Little Rock. He also federalized the Arkansas National Guard, taking it out of the governor's hands, so that the soldiers could protect the black students and enforce integration. Thus, the Little Rock Nine were able to attend school on Wednesday, September 25, 1957. However, they continued to be subjected to abuse—physical and verbal—by many of the school's white students.

Pictured here is Elizabeth Eckford, one of the Little Rock Nine, on September 4, 1957, being verbally abused by a young woman as she attempts to enter the school.

The desegregation of Little Rock Central High School is one of the most significant events in the Civil Rights Movement.

Soldiers of the 101st Airborne Division of the U.S. Army push white students away with their rifles so that the Little Rock Nine may safely enter Central High School.

Four black students attempt to enter North Little Rock High School on September 10, 1957. No National Guardsmen were present, but the police escorted the black students away after a mob hurling taunts and threats prevented them from entering.

A black girl is protected by a National Guardsman as she makes her way to Little Rock High School in 1957.

A high school in Norfolk, Virginia, Norview Senior High, is integrated in February of 1959. Here two of five black students assigned to this previously all-white school are surrounded by students and journalists as they enter the building.

Patricia Turner, one of the five black students registered at Norview Senior High School, sits in class among her fellow students.

Police officers in Jackson, Mississippi, escort a group of black students out of the Jackson Public Library after they had entered the main library building, which was reserved for white use only.

Four black college students held a sit-in at a Woolworth's lunch counter in Greensboro, North Carolina, in February of 1960. The sit-in was a peaceful protest and part of a series of sit-ins that led to policy change by the store and increased national awareness of the Civil Rights Movement. This Woolworth's store is now the International Civil Rights Center and Museum. On the first day of the sit-in, the four men ordered coffee, but were refused service at the "Whites Only" counter and asked to leave by the store's manager. The next day, twenty more students joined the original Greensboro Four. While the black students were taunted by white customers, they remained at the lunch counter, reading and studying quietly. The press covered this day of protest, and with each consecutive day, more black protesters appeared at the sit-in. Still, Woolworth's declined to serve the black students. This movement spread to other cities throughout the South, and the sit-ins continued. Finally, black students began a boycott of stores that had segregated lunch counters, and after sales at these stores dropped significantly, the managers and owners at last agreed to abandon their segregationist policies.

On July 25, 1960, black employees of the Greensboro Woolworth's were the first to be served at the store's lunch counter. The entire Woolworth's chain was desegregated the next day.

The tension at a lunch counter in Portsmouth, Virginia, is nearly visible in the minutes before a fight broke out between white students and black youths who sought service at this previously segregated cafeteria.

Protesters march for civil rights on August 28, 1963, at the March on Washington, a landmark demonstration of the Civil Rights Movement.

Thurgood Marshall walks out of the Supreme Court building.

Jackie Robinson, American baseball player and hero of the Civil Rights Movement.

Reverend Martin Luther King, Jr., in his office in Atlanta, Georgia, where a photograph of Mahatma Gandhi hangs. Gandhi's discipline of nonviolent protest inspired King and his followers.

Rosa Parks, who is sometimes known as the "Mother of the Civil Rights Movement," touched off the Montgomery, Alabama, bus boycott in December 1955, after she refused to give up her seat on a city bus to a white passenger.

Mary McLeod Bethune with First Lady Eleanor Roosevelt. The two were close friends.

Claudette Colvin was the first person of color to protest bus segregation, refusing to give up her seat to a white person on a bus in Montgomery, Alabama, at the age of fifteen. She was taken off the bus and arrested by two police officers.

Ruby Bridges was the first black child to integrate a previously all-white elementary school, when she attended the William Frantz Elementary School in New Orleans, Louisiana, at the age of six.

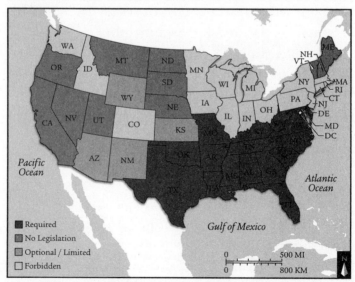

A map of the continental United States showing the legality of school segregation state by state, before the Supreme Court's ruling in Brown v. Board of Education of Topeka.

Real People Mentioned in Dawnie Rae's Diary

Mary McLeod Bethune Mary was an educator who founded Bethune-Cookman University in Daytona Beach, Florida. This college began as an all-black grade school. Legend says that Mary earned money to keep the school going by baking and selling sweet potato pies. Mary worked to get President Franklin D. Roosevelt elected. The president appointed her as a member of his Black Cabinet. In this role, Mary advised the president on the concerns of African Americans.

Harry F. Byrd Byrd was elected the fiftieth governor of Virginia. He later became a U.S. senator, who exercised his political power to oppose school integration. Byrd's Massive Resistance program worked to maintain segregation in schools throughout Virginia, forcing them to close by withdrawing funds. Though Byrd had many followers, his Massive Resistance did not last.

Claudette Colvin In 1955, Claudette was fifteen years old. She was a student at Booker T. Washington High School in Montgomery, Alabama, where she lived. Like many residents of Montgomery, Claudette rode segregated city buses. On March 2, 1955, Claudette refused to give up her seat on the bus to a white person. This courageous act occurred nine months before Rosa Parks took the same brave action by also refusing to give up her seat on a Montgomery, Alabama, bus.

George E. C. Hayes George Edward Chalmers Hayes was a Washington, D.C., lawyer who was a leader in arguing *Bolling v. Sharpe*, a case similar to *Brown v. Board of Education*.

Martin Luther King, Jr. Martin Luther King, Jr., was one of the foremost civil rights leaders of all time. A clergyman and social activist, King became known throughout the world for his beliefs and teachings of nonviolence in the face of America's turbulent racial segregation of the 1950s and 1960s. King is perhaps best remembered for his landmark "I Have a Dream" speech delivered at the March on Washington in 1963. In 1964, King was the youngest person to receive the Nobel Peace Prize for his work to end racial inequality.

Thurgood Marshall Marshall was an attorney who started his career working for the National Association for the Advancement of Colored People (NAACP). He later argued before the Supreme Court on the *Brown v. Board of Education* case. This experience prepared Marshall to become the first African American to serve on the Supreme Court of the United States.

James M. Nabrit Nabrit was a leading civil rights lawyer who worked with George E. C. Hayes on the *Bolling v. Sharpe* case. Nabrit also served as an attorney on several cases for the NAACP Legal Defense and Educational Fund.

Jackie Robinson Jack Roosevelt "Jackie" Robinson was the first black player in Major League Baseball in modern history. Jackie broke baseball's invisible "color line" in 1947 when he first appeared as a player for the Brooklyn Dodgers. For sixty years before Jackie debuted with the Dodgers, black baseball players could only play for the Negro Leagues. Thanks to Jackie, racial segregation in professional baseball came to an end.

Thomas B. Stanley   Stanley served as governor of Virginia from 1954–1958, during the height of the school integration controversy. Shortly after the *Brown v. Board of Education* ruling, Stanley encouraged the people of Virginia to accept integration. But he was soon swayed by Virginia's strong segregationists' beliefs, and by the powerful strategies set forth by Harry F. Byrd's Massive Resistance program.

About Negro History Week

Negro History Week was created by historian Carter G. Woodson to bring national attention to the achievements of black people in America. Woodson chose the second week of February for Negro History Week because it marks the birthdays of Frederick Douglass and Abraham Lincoln.

Negro History Week became Black History Month in 1976, and in recent years has been renamed African American History Month.

Civil Rights Timeline

Here are important civil rights events that would have happened during Dawnie Rae's lifetime.

1954   May 17   The Supreme Court rules against segregation in public schools in the landmark case *Brown v. Board of Education of Topeka.*

1955   August 28   Emmett Louis Till, a fourteen-year-old boy from Mississippi, is lynched for supposedly whistling at a white woman. The crime draws widespread media attention.

December 1   Rosa Parks, an African American seamstress from Montgomery, Alabama, refuses to give up her seat to a white man at the front of a segregated bus. This act of bravery ignites the Montgomery Bus Boycotts. African Americans refuse to ride city buses for more than one year. After a Supreme Court ruling on December 21, 1956, Montgomery, Alabama, buses are desegregated.

1957   January–February   The Southern

Christian Leadership Conference (SCLC) is established with the help of Dr. Martin Luther King, Jr., who becomes the SCLC's first president. The SCLC promotes nonviolence as a means for social change.

September The Little Rock Nine, a group of black students in Little Rock, Arkansas, enroll in Central High School, an all-white school. Arkansas governor Orval Faubus prevents the students from entering the school. The students are allowed to enter when President Dwight D. Eisenhower sends the National Guard to protect them.

1960 February 1 Four African American college freshmen sit at a segregated Woolworth's lunch counter in Greensboro, North Carolina. They refuse to leave the counter until they are served. As a result, the Greensboro sit-ins begin, and spark sit-ins throughout the nation.

April Activist Ella Baker helps form the Student Nonviolent Coordinating Committee (SNCC) at Shaw University in North Carolina. The group's purpose is to help young people organize peaceful civil rights demonstrations.

1961 May 4 Thousands of student volunteers begin "Freedom Rides" throughout the South. To test laws that prohibit segregation, these young people, black and white, travel on buses together. The students must endure violence. They are supported by SNCC and the Congress on Racial Equality (CORE).

1962 October 1 James Meredith is the first African American student to enroll at the University of Mississippi. James is met by angry mobs. President John F. Kennedy sends 5,000 federal troops to help.

1963 April 16 Dr. Martin Luther King, Jr., writes his "Letter from Birmingham Jail" after being arrested and put in jail during a protest in Birmingham, Alabama. His letter outlines the meaning of justice.

August 28 Nearly 250,000 people gather at the Lincoln Memorial as part of the March on Washington. Dr. Martin Luther King, Jr., delivers his world-famous "I Have a Dream" speech.

1964 July 2 President Lyndon B. Johnson signs the Civil Rights Act of 1964, which outlaws racial segregation in public places.

About the Author

Andrea Davis Pinkney is the *New York Times* best-selling and award-winning author of many books for children and young adults, including picture books, novels, works of historical fiction, and nonfiction.

She is the author of several notable titles, including the historical fiction novel *Bird in a Box* and the nonfiction picture books *Sit-In: How Four Friends Stood Up By Sitting Down*, a Parents' Choice Award winner and winner of the Carter G. Woodson Award for historical works for young people; *Sojourner Truth's Step-Stomp Stride*, a Jane Addams Honor Book and *School Library Journal* Best Book of the Year; the Coretta Scott King Author Honor Book *Let it Shine: Stories of Black Women Freedom Fighters*; *Duke Ellington*, a Caldecott Honor and Coretta Scott King Honor Book; and *Boycott Blues: How Rosa Parks Inspired a Nation*, winner of the Anne Izard Storyteller's Choice Award. Andrea was named one of the "25 Most Influential

People in Our Children's Lives" by *Children's Health Magazine.*

She lives in New York City with her husband and frequent collaborator, award-winning illustrator Brian Pinkney, and their two children.

About writing *With the Might of Angels*, Andrea says, "I come from a long line of civil rights activists, the closest to me being my late father, Philip J. Davis. In 1959 Dad was selected as one of the first African American student interns in the U.S. House of Representatives. He was later named by the White House as the U.S. deputy assistant secretary of labor and director of the office of federal contract compliance.

"In this role, Dad became the prime author of federal affirmative action legislation. Additionally, he advised several presidential administrations on the legalities of fair labor practices for African Americans and women.

"When I was six years old, Dad enrolled me in first grade at an all-white elementary school, where I was the only black student. (Mom was a teacher at a school in another district, so it was Dad's job to escort me to Mrs. Lewis's class.)

"Recently, in speaking to my mom about my

experience of going to an all-white grade school, I asked if Dad had any involvement in the legislation surrounding school integration or the *Brown v. Board of Education* Supreme Court ruling. Mom's first answer was no, but she then dug through Dad's personal belongings and memorabilia from his days on Capitol Hill, and found a weighty three-ring binder from a civil rights conference Dad had attended. The notebook's cover was marked **BROWN V. BOARD OF EDUCATION — 'Confronting the Promise.'** The gathering of civil rights leaders commemorated the fortieth anniversary of *Brown v. Board of Education*. It had been held in Williamsburg, Virginia, and focused on school integration in the state of Virginia.

"Dad's family is originally from Culpeper, Virginia, and he was always very proud of this. He took great care in learning about Virginia's history, politics, and the legacy of African Americans in Virginia.

"I pored over the binder's pages, a comprehensive collection of materials Dad had saved, including news articles, litigation documents, magazine editorials on school integration, copies of archival photographs, state maps, and more.

"The notebook was divided into tabbed sections. There was one entitled 'The Virginia Experience,' which contained an assortment of articles about school integration written in the mid 1950s and early 1960s. These were published in *U.S. News & World Report*, the *Saturday Evening Post*, *Newsweek*, and other publications.

"(Like Dawnie's daddy, my own father was an avid reader of newspapers and periodicals. And, he collected documents and papers that were of special interest to him.)

"The pages in Dad's binder whopped me on the head like a two-by-four — they told such a compelling story!

"Though I'd attended the all-white elementary school more than a decade after the *Brown v. Board of Education* decision, I still felt a keen sense of loneliness and isolation as the school's only black student. I didn't experience the torment Dawnie did, but was plagued by a phenomenon I've come to call 'anxious apartness.'

"As a child, I could not fully understand or articulate these feelings, but they were very real.

"Dad's collection of materials and my own school experience compelled me to craft a school integration story for today's readers.

"Dawnie Rae Johnson's diary is a fictionalized account of the events surrounding school integration in the state of Virginia. Dawnie's narrative is inspired by several harrowing integration stories, including that of my own cousin John Mullen, who, as a direct result of the *Brown v. Board of Education* ruling, integrated Homer L. Ferguson High School in Newport News, Virginia. I also spoke to others who shared similar struggles and triumphs at school.

"Integration at the Fort Myer military base in Virginia serves as the model for this book's fictional town, Hadley, which, for the purposes of this story, is set in Lee County, a real county in the state of Virginia.

"In order to align the dates of Dawnie's diary with the day upon which the *Brown v. Board of Education* ruling happened, I've begun her story in May 1954.

"Though most schools did not integrate at that time, I felt it important to directly link the *Brown v. Board of Education* decision with immediate school integration, so that young readers could connect the two. Also, setting the diary narratives in 1954–1955 enabled the story to include pivotal civil rights and historical events that occurred during that time, and that had a direct effect on school integration.

"Although this diary is a work of fiction, many of the events cited actually happened on the dates they occur in the book. These include the *Brown v. Board of Education* Supreme Court ruling, the appointment of Governor Thomas B. Stanley's Commission on Public Education, the formation of the Defenders of State Sovereignty and Individual Liberties, the Montgomery, Alabama, bus protest of young Claudette Colvin, the premiere of *Sports Illustrated* magazine, and the folding of the All-American Girls Professional Baseball League. The facts about Jackie Robinson are also true.

"While the appearance of Martin Luther King, Jr., at Dawnie's church is fiction, young Martin visited many different churches throughout the South, where he encouraged members to become registered voters and active members of the NAACP. He also preached the importance of nonviolence.

"In 1954, Martin became pastor of the Dexter Avenue Baptist Church in Montgomery, Alabama. It was at this time that his career as a preacher and civil rights leader began to gain public recognition.

"The Sutter's Dairy Boycott is also fictional, though in December 1955, Martin Luther King, Jr., led the historic Montgomery Bus Boycott, ignited by Rosa Parks's refusal to give up her seat on a segregated city bus.

"Although I was the only black student at my very first grade school, my experience was not nearly as harsh as Dawnie's. I've often asked myself if I could have endured what Dawnie suffered. Thankfully, like Dawnie, I am rooted in a strong family whose loving arms got me through the loneliest times.

"I wrote this book to remind young readers of the great privilege they enjoy — that of attending any school they wish, with classmates of all races — and to show them that even in the harshest situations, hope can shine through the darkest days."

Acknowledgments

Like Dawnie Rae, I was blessed "with the might of angels" in the creation of this book. Special thanks to Katherine Wilkins, reference librarian, Virginia Historical Society, whose careful attention to the details involving school integration and legislation in the state of Virginia helped me solidify and round out the facts in Dawnie's narrative.

I thank my cousin John Mullen, whose colorful recounting of his own integration experiences in Newport News, Virginia, gave life to Dawnie's story and that of her family. Thanks, too, to Rhonda Joy McLean, who integrated her school in Smithfield, North Carolina, and who generously shared her memories with me.

Thank you, all my friends and colleagues at Scholastic for inviting Dawnie Rae Johnson into the Dear America fold, and for fostering a love of history through the Dear America series.

Elizabeth Parisi, special thanks to you for designing such an engaging book cover. Thanks, too, to artist Tim O'Brien for your portrait depicting Dawnie with beauty and dignity. Thank you, Elizabeth Starr Baer, for your amazing copyediting talents and your eagle-eyed fact-checking of the material.

Rebecca Sherman, my agent, and Lisa Sandell, my editor, you are both angels without whose might I could not have written this book. I thank you for your keen editorial insights, and for the care with which you each helped me polish Dawnie's story.

Thanks to Mom, for being the keeper of memories, and for somehow always managing to pull the right rabbit from the right hat, at the right moment.

Finally, thanks to the angels who live under the same roof as I do — my daughter, Chloe, and son, Dobbin, who listened to Dawnie's story for months and offered invaluable suggestions for making her real.

Finally, a loving thank-you to my brightest angel of all, Brian Pinkney, for reading each and every one of this diary's entries, for laughing in all the right places, and for helping me bring power and grace to Dawnie Rae and the Johnson family.

Grateful acknowledgment is made for permission to use the following:

Cover portrait by Tim O'Brien.

Cover background: High School, Library of Congress (LC-D4-71582).

Page 50: George E. C. Hayes, Thurgood Marshall, and James M. Nabrit outside the Supreme Court, AP Photo.

Page 303 (top): Sign for Colored Dining Room on an outhouse, Esther Bubley/Bettmann/Corbis.

Page 303 (bottom): "Colored Only" sign on water fountain, Bettmann/Corbis.

Page 304: One of the Little Rock Nine, being verbally abused as she attempts to enter the school, ullstein bild/The Image Works.

Page 305 (top): Soldiers of 101st Airborne Division push white students away for the safety of the Little Rock Nine, in Central High School, SZ Photo/The Image Works.

Page 305 (bottom): Black students attempt to enter North Little Rock High School, Clyde Priest/Bettmann/Corbis.

Page 306: A black girl protected by a National Guardsman as she enters Little Rock High School, Topham/The Image Works.

Page 307 (top): Two black students entering Norview Senior High in Norfolk, Virginia, AP Photo.

Page 307 (bottom): A black student in class in Norfolk, Virginia, ibid.

Page 308: Police officers escorting black students out of the Jackson Public Library, Jackson, Mississippi, ibid.

Page 309: Four black students sit-in at lunch counter to protest segregation, Jack Moebes/Corbis.

Page 310 (top): Tension at a segregated lunch cafeteria as black students ask for service, AP Photo.

Page 310 (bottom): March on Washington for civil rights, August 28, 1963, Wally McNamee/Corbis.

Page 311: Thurgood Marshall, foreground, left, walking out of the Supreme Court, Donald Uhrbrock/Time Life Pictures/Getty Images.

Page 312: Jackie Robinson, Roger-Viollet/The Image Works.

Page 313: Martin Luther King, Jr., in his office with photo of Mahatma Gandhi, Bob Fitch/Take Stock/The Image Works.

Page 314: Rosa Parks, Paul Schutzer/Time Life Pictures/Getty Images.

Page 315 (top): Mary McLeod Bethune with Eleanor Roosevelt, Topham/The Image Works.

Page 315 (bottom): Claudette Colvin, AP Photo.

Page 316 (top): Ruby Bridges, ibid.

Page 316 (bottom): Map by Jim McMahon.

Other books in the Dear America series

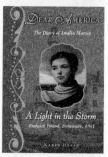

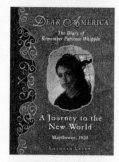